Secret obsession makes for the sweet

Overwhelmed by her new life in another era with the Laird of Gealach, and the feelings that threaten to consume her, Emma determines she must return to her own time and a semblance of sanity. Having heard of a magical circle of stones atop the ridge overlooking Loch Ness, she manages to escape from the castle and the desire and intensity of Logan that's held her captive.

When Logan realizes Emma is missing, he is enraged and terrified. He seeks to find her and when he does, he will punish her exquisitely for leaving him, and for inexplicably exposing his scorching fascination and adoration.

Together again, their passions are reignited and a new stunning level of sensuality and self-discovery invoked. But underneath it all, both still wrestle with their inner demons and the impending danger of angered clans and traitors among them. Revealing how they feel about each other could bring about cataclysmic crash within their hearts and the realm. The blade is sharp on both edges, but they know not which side to choose, for one promises sweet, decadent surrender and the other, irrevocable damage—and they aren't certain which is which. Will baring her soul to the Highlander forever change the course of history?

Praise for *BEHIND THE PLAID*
(Book One: Highland Bound Trilogy)

4 ½ stars and a Top Pick from Night Owl Romance! *"Wickedly sinful, arousingly erotic, and delightfully delicious, Logan is the stuff that naughty Highlander dreams are made of."*

Bared to the Laird

Bared to the Laird
Book Two – Highland Bound Trilogy

By
Eliza Knight

****
FIRST EDITION
August 2013

Cover Design by Kimberly Killion @ The Killion Group, Inc.

ISBN-13: 978-1492136828
ISBN-10: 1492136824

****

Also Available by Eliza Knight

The Rebound Pact – A Sexy Contemporary
The Highlander's Reward – Book One, The Stolen Bride Series
The Highlander's Conquest – Book Two, The Stolen Bride Series
The Highlander's Lady – Book Three, The Stolen Bride Series
The Highlander's Warrior Bride – Book Four, The Stolen Bride Series
The Highlander's Triumph – Book Five, The Stolen Bride Series
A Lady's Charade (Book 1: The Rules of Chivalry)
A Knight's Victory (Book 2: The Rules of Chivalry)
A Gentleman's Kiss
<u>*Men of the Sea Series:*</u> *Her Captain Returns, Her Captain Surrenders, Her Captain Dares All*
<u>*The Highland Jewel Series:*</u> *Warrior in a Box, Lady in a Box, Love in a Box*
Lady Seductress's Ball
Take it Off, Warrior
Highland Steam
A Pirate's Bounty
Highland Tryst (Something Wicked This Way Comes Volume 1)
Highlander Brawn (Sequel to Highland Steam)

Coming soon…

The Dark Side of the Laird (Book 3: Highland Bound)
The Highlander's Sin (Book 6: The Stolen Bride Series)

Writing under the name E. Knight

Coming soon…

My Lady Viper – Tales From the Tudor Court
Prisoner of the Queen – Tales From the Tudor Court

Writing under the name Annabelle Weston

Wicked Woman (Desert Heat)

Scandalous Woman (Desert Heat)
Notorious Woman (Desert Heat)
Mr. Temptation
Hunting Tucker

****

Visit Eliza Knight at <u>www.elizaknight.com</u> or <u>www.historyundressed.com</u>

Dedication

To my amazing husband, who reads my books without batting an eye and encourages me to let my imagination soar.

Acknowledgements

Many special thanks to the following people for their help in preparing this book: Jennifer Bray-Weber, Tara Kingston, Andrea Snyder, Lizzie Walker and Kimberly Killion.

CHAPTER ONE

Emma

Scottish Highlands
Early Fall, 1542

"**I** am a time traveler."

A shiver stole over me as the words I'd held suppressed for so long tumbled across my tongue. Not having uttered those five words aloud before, they felt foreign on my lips. Unnatural. A lie.

I bit the inside of my cheek and put a little more *oomph* into the statement. Hoping that though I sounded like a fraud to myself, I wouldn't sound that way to the one person I wanted to believe me. "Logan, I'm not from here. I am from the future."

Inside I groaned. Anyway I put it was going to sound awkward and a bit psychotic. What would I say next, that a bolt of lightning and touching the stones of his gate—spires that

9

were not there yet because they wouldn't be built for several hundred years—had somehow magically whisked me back in time?

It was the truth. It had happened. But there was no way in hell he was going to believe me. The truth sounded ludicrous. And I didn't really fancy seeing myself in the dungeon.

Swiping a hand through the tangles in my wavy red hair, I turned to stare up at the cracks in the plaster of the ceiling. Thank goodness Logan was not truly in my bedroom. My confession was going to be a disaster.

I had no way of telling what day it was, or how long I'd been there, but I'd tried to keep count. Waking up each morning and adding a day onto the last. Today was one-hundred twenty-three. I think. Just over four months since I'd arrived at Gealach Castle, and I could still feel the spark on my fingertips, radiating up my arms. Still sense the confusion of that morning, waking up in the warm, dry grass. A battle was quickly ensuing around me. Remembering only that it had been night, and storming, and recalling nothing of how I'd gotten there, or how I'd fallen asleep. The very air had pressed in and out, vibrating. And I remembered meeting Logan.

Not the most coordinated moments of my life—I'd fallen down the front stairs of his castle, and gazed up at the most tall, dark and handsome fantasies a woman could dream up. Hair as dark as midnight and eyes as fierce as storm clouds. Skin tanned and taut. My mouth had watered...still watered.

Every time I see him, it's as though for the first time. My body surges to life, every cell and nerve reaching out to him. Wanting him to touch me, caress me, hold me.

Back in present day somewhere, Steven—could I even think of him as my husband?—probably still searched for me. I don't think he'd ever stop. He was obsessed, and I'd let myself be drug down into the mire that was his abusive mantra. Believed I was nothing, no one. Fate had somehow intervened and brought me here. To Logan. To Gealach. To a place where I feared not for my safety from the man who I trusted with my heart, soul, but outside forces.

The room darkened, and I turned toward the window, shutters open to let in a morning breeze. A dark cloud blew across the sun, hiding the light. Another storm was churning, darkening the sky and hiding the pretty blue. They'd been coming more and more frequently. Prompting my need to tell Logan the truth about where I'd come from, in case one of these storms sent me back to my own time. A fear I'd had all along. At first, I'd wanted it, pined for it. Now, I wasn't so sure.

Below in the courtyard, the inhabitants of Gealach — the fearsome Grant clan — went about their daily routines. Carting baskets of goods. Blacksmiths hammering out metal things. Stable boys working with horses. Children tugging buckets to the well. Their faces were lined with strain as they wearily glanced about them. Over the past several months, the lines had grown deeper, the furtive glances more frequent. The chief of Clan MacDonald — mortal enemy to the Grant clan, to Logan — had made it back to the northern isles alive. A feat of pure hatred and willpower, I'm sure, after Logan tied him to the mast of the man's own ship, shackled with the iron manacles he'd brought to enslave the people of Gealach.

MacDonald had yet to retaliate, and the only reason we knew he'd made it back was because news of Logan's daring move traveled swiftly through the Highlands. A giddy excitement and fear took hold and sent children scurrying with the slightest shift in the wind and warriors to grab hold of their weapons. An underlying tension shadowed over the castle. Everyone knew MacDonald was coming. We just didn't know when. A medieval day apocalypse. But as much as it scared me, I had faith in Logan that he could kick MacDonald's ass again.

Logan was the King of Scotland's own man. The Guardian of Scotland. But that didn't matter to a maniac like MacDonald.

He wanted his revenge—and the king's seat. It was about power. About ripping apart a man who'd bested him. Not just because in this dark sixteenth century war itched to be released from every man's sword. There were men like him in every century.

My ex-husband was a man like that. He preyed on the weak, and I'd been the prey. Logan set me free—mostly. I was still holding back. Waiting for the curtain to drop and every time a cloud covered the sun I swore it was going to end. That lightning would strike and I'd wake up at home in Steven's bed. Sinking back into the nightmare I'd fled from.

Thunder cracked, startling me from my thoughts. My gaze went from the people below back to the sky.

The clouds were light and dark grey swirls, shaping worlds in the sky. The sun burned to come through, reaching through every hole it could find. Almost as if the universe fought for me—keeping the storms at bay. The successful rays of sunlight beamed down in stripes hitting the courtyard, the moors and the sea beyond.

A swift knock at the door that connected mine and Logan's two bedrooms had me jerking away from the window. I yelped when my elbow bumped against the stone casement. Biting my lip, I rubbed the spot and watched as Logan swept open the door and stepped through.

Rugged. Dark. Wicked.

When he walked into a room every woman lost her breath and grew weak in the knees. Since I was the only woman here, I didn't have to glower at any simpering females either. He had all of my attention.

And damn, if I hadn't lost my breath and grown weak in the knees.

His dark eyes pierced mine. A shadow of stubble covered his chin. Hair pulled back and tied with a leather thong. Plaid pleated around his hips, flung over his shoulder and beneath it a crisp linen shirt that clung to the muscles of his biceps, shoulders and chest. My mouth watered and it wasn't the only thing that got wet.

"Logan," I said, my breath catching as it did every time he came in.

Now was my chance. I had to tell him the truth. The risk. I opened my mouth to tell him we needed to talk, but he spoke first.

"Emma." His Scottish brogue never grew old. A natural aphrodisiac. He glanced around as though he expected his demons to leap from the mortar between the stones. "Someone has been watching us."

There were always people watching. Logan had bade my main maid Agatha, and the other servants who helped me to keep quiet about our relationship. None other than them, and Ewan—Logan's second in command—was aware that I was Logan's lover. Just a guest. Though, I was sure at this point they suspected. "What do you mean? Has Agatha not been discreet?"

Logan shook his head. "Nay, 'tis not that. I found this outside my door this morning." He held up the sheer black nightgown I'd worn at least a dozen times for Logan. Sexy medieval lingerie that I'd had to work up the nerve to slide over my skin, only to have him pull it off again. Shredded.

I bit my lip. "Maybe they dropped it on the way to the laundry and a cat got into it?"

Logan frowned, a look so fearsome I shuddered. "Nay. Look." He lifted the nightgown with two hands, showing me that the fabric had multiple slashes. Looked like the work of a blade rather than claws and teeth.

My mouth opened in shock, a gasp choking me. I stepped forward, reaching for the destroyed garment. Gooseflesh rose over my arms, and a shiver of fear raced up my spine. Someone didn't like me. Or my relationship with Logan. Either way, it was a clear threat. I'd have been gutted if I wore it when the offending attacker hit.

"Who would do such a thing?" I asked, unable to take my eyes off the ruined garment.

Logan wouldn't let me take the nightgown. He flung it into the hearth, lit the flint and set it on fire. We both stared silently at the flames as they swiftly consumed the flimsy material, melting it into ash. Nothing left of something that held so much power. The gown had put fear inside me the first time I saw it. Then it had given me strength when I finally got the nerve to slip into it. And finally, the sheer magical nightgown had the power to make Logan quake when he saw me in it, every inch of my body exposed, and yet not, to his vision.

"I dinna know. But if they are watching and figured out what we've been doing, they are not the only ones. We need to be more discreet. There are too many risks involved."

I pushed aside my feelings of inadequacy. He wasn't hiding me because he was embarrassed. It was for both our safety; the welfare of the kingdom was at stake.

I nodded. How much more discreet could we be? In the open we didn't touch. Barely spoke. At night, and maybe a stolen moment during the day, we made love. There were only a few who knew, and they were supposedly trustworthy. I wore a ring he'd given me the month before. A band of gold with an iridescent seashell. It was one we'd found while on a walk. A perfectly tiny, heart-shaped shell. But no one knew of the ring, except for maybe the man who'd fashioned it. "Do you think it was Agatha or one of the other maids? Ewan? The ring maker?"

He shook his head. "Your maids have been with me for a long time. They fear reprisal more than a cash payout from MacDonald. The ring maker, he'd no idea who I gave it to, and besides, he wouldn't have dared tell. And Ewan is like a brother to me. He'd never betray me."

Ewan was like a brother to me, too—which sounded odd considering I'd supposedly only known him a few months. But his resemblance was uncanny to my own brother, who was presumed dead along with my parents, in a plane crash over the Atlantic. His mannerisms, the way we'd bonded, it was like he was indeed my brother.

"More troubling," he turned to face me, "is that they came into your room to get the garment. Tore it up and then left it outside my door for anyone to happen on it."

"My room isn't locked. Anyone could have come in." I tried to reason it out, but that didn't matter. Whether the door was locked or not, someone came in with nefarious purpose.

Murder filled his eyes, and I was glad I hadn't been the one to cross him. "Nobody touches what's mine. I will find out who did this. They will be punished."

Logan was too tense. Muscles bunched, arms crossed, brows knitted together, lips turned down. I reached out to touch him, stroking my fingers over his arm. The tension didn't melt but it did lessen. He pulled me into his arms and kissed me. At first a gentle brush of his lips on mine. Don't hold back, I wanted to say. I flicked my tongue over the seam of his lips, an invitation to delve deeper. His grip on me tightened and he growled.

Liquid heat pooled deep inside me, pleasure radiating from the center outward. Every part of me strained for him to make love to me. To erase the fact that someone was very displeased with our actions. His tongue swept in, taking possession, claiming me as he always did, and I opened up, letting him take me.

I wrapped my arms around his middle, making my body flush to his, feeling the contours of his muscles, the hardness of his erection, as he pressed into me.

Logan's hands threaded through my hair, massaging my scalp, and his chest rumbled with his appreciation. I pressed my pelvis hard against his, telling him what I wanted, amazed by how much he'd changed me.

Sex used to be something I feared. The pain Steven inflicted every time we did it remained not quite a distant memory, but one that was fading. Logan was filling up the rest of the space. Filling it with delicious, wonderful memories that helped to heal the pain of my past. A past I'd just as soon forget.

Behind my closed lids, I sensed the room brightening. I opened my eyes, seeing Logan's piercing dark gaze. They reminded me of onyx stones, but when he was kissing me, making love to me, they glowed like coals.

Tingles of need gripped me, making my nipples ache, my sex slick and spasming.

The light was from the sun—the clouds had rolled on. A breeze blew through the open window. The universe seemed to have won another day. No storm, yet. But that didn't matter. I had to tell him.

Pulling away a couple inches, I whispered, "I have to talk to you about something."

"What is it?" he whispered, breaking eye contact to lay a path of searing kisses down my neck.

"I..." God, I couldn't talk. Not with the way his tongue flicked wickedly over my pulse. I just wanted to hike up my gown, his plaid and wrap my legs around him, feel him sink inside me. "Mmm."

That sinful tongue slid over my collarbone. Strong, coarse fingers tugged at the neck of my gown, grazing tantalizingly over the top of my breast. I lost my train of thought as his lips skimmed over my taut nipple, exposed to the heat of his mouth. I arched my back, wanting more, knowing that he was distracting me from something very important.

"No, wait," I said hoarsely. "I have to tell you."

"Tell me," he teased, exposing my other nipple and drawing it into his mouth.

I couldn't think. Couldn't form words. Couldn't do anything but scrape my fingers through his hair and tug him closer.

"I'm not from here," I managed. My body was on fire, desire leaping from every inch of my skin. I reached between us and gripped his hard cock, covered by the pleats of his plaid. That was what I wanted. This, inside me. We could talk later.

"I know," he said. His tugged at the bottom of my gown, filling his fist full of fabric. "You are from the new world."

That much I'd told him, yes. But the era... Well...

Cool air blew over my naked thigh, quickly warmed by the stroke of his hand.

I groaned as he slid his fingers up my inner thigh and stroked lightly over the wetness of my cunt.

"Aye..." he growled against the flesh of my hard nipples. "Ye're ready for me."

"You don't understand," I said softly, sucking my lower lip into my mouth.

"This, I understand very well." He plunged his fingers deep.

I cried out. Oh, yeah he understood...

His thumb swirled over my clit, fingers plunged inside, stroking me into a frenzy. The man had no idea how much he affected me. I was addicted. Obsessed. Willing to let go of that important piece of information he needed, just to feel what he did to me. To enjoy the wickedness of his touch. Anticipating what new delight he'd introduce to me.

Logan turned me around, stroking my clit with one hand and gripping the exposed flesh of my breast with the other. He walked me forward, until the tips of my toes pressed the stone wall at the base of the tiny window. I could see outside. See the sun shining. See the people below going about their duties.

And I was excited all the more.

Could they see me?

I'd never known myself to be an exhibitionist... But with Logan I was always finding out new things about myself.

"Do ye see them all?" he whispered in my ear, teeth scraping over my neck. He pinched my nipple. Hard.

I gasped. "Yes."

"Do ye think they can see ye?"

He plunged his fingers inside me, coating himself in my cream. The muscles of my core clenched tight to his fingers. Not wanting to let him go. But he slowly slid them out, guiding one pad over the swollen bundle of nerves that sparked with each ensuing stroke. I could barely think, let alone talk.

"Do ye think they know what I'm doing to ye?"

I tried to think about when I'd been below, staring up at the imposing walls of Gealach. Could I see into the windows?

"I...I don't know," I whispered. Part of me found the idea of others watching thrilling, but the logical side—the side that was being subdued by pleasure—knew it would be damaging.

"I thought we were supposed..." God I couldn't get the words to pass over my tongue. "Supposed...to be careful." The last word faded on a moan when he gently bit the side of my neck as he plucked my nipple and expertly tapped my clit.

"They canna see us. But we can see them. Let this be another lesson, lass... A lesson in..." He groaned.

My breast grew cold as he moved the heat of his hand to the small of my back, forcing me to bend forward. I braced myself on the window casing—luckily over a foot deep so my head didn't hang outside. Cool wind touched my ass as he yanked up my gown.

A tender smack. I bit my lip.

"I'm going to fuck ye while ye watch the world move around ye like nothing so sinful was happening."

I closed my eyes, the images he put inside my mind overwhelming. A fresh rush of fluid drenched my sex, and I pushed my buttocks back, silently begging him to take me.

Every time we made love, there was a lesson learned. Either a new way we moved, a new place, a new instrument, a new way of thinking. This was new. This was… Fucking amazing.

"Tell me ye want it, Emma."

I shivered. Couldn't get enough of his demands.

"I want it."

A gentle breeze blew over my bared behind, a rustle of fabric, and then the heat of his cock head probed my tingling flesh. The strength of his thighs, warm, bristly, taut pressed to the back of my legs. With the toe of his boot he nudged my legs wider.

"Good God, lass, ye are beautiful. Always ready for me."

He slid the crown of his cock over my clit, through my wet folds to the drenched slit, craving what was about to come. I pushed back just when he slid his cock up, so that he sank in a fraction of an inch.

"Eager, are ye?" He chuckled and playfully slapped at my ass again. "I am, too." The latter was said in a gruff whisper against the back of my neck as he plunged deep inside me.

I cried out as the thickness of his cock stretched me. Then I swiftly brought my hand up to cover my lips. Anyone below could have heard me.

"Just a cry on the wind, nothing more, nothing less," he crooned.

Logan slid out, inch by torturous inch, before plunging back inside. He held a strong grip on one hip, and the other made light, teasing circles over my clit. My thighs trembled, fingers dug into the stone casement. My breath came out in pants.

I turned my head as far as I could, taking in the sight of my brawny Highlander, black eyes heavily lidded with passion, and trained on me.

"Kiss me," I said, wanting to feel his warm lips on mine.

He plunged harder, deeper. Bent over and claimed my lips. I let go of the casement with one hand to slide my palm up around the back of his neck, holding him to me, as I drew his tongue into my mouth.

The harder I kissed him, the more demanding with my tongue, the harder he fucked me. His fingers dug into the sides of my hip, making me wonder if tomorrow there'd be bruises. Love wounds. A battle of passion.

I rolled my hips, arching my back to take him in deeper. He no longer teased my clit, but rubbed it in earnest, knowing just the right amount of pressure and movement to make me come.

I was so close, almost there, my body coiling tight, flashes of ecstasy rushing through my veins. I couldn't hold back. Didn't want to.

Orgasm took over. Abducting my senses. I moaned into Logan's mouth, and he roared into mine. Our stifled cries, and heated push and pull overpowering. Warmth filled me as Logan plunged deep one final time, filling me up with his climax.

Just when I thought it couldn't get any better… It always did.

CHAPTER TWO

Logan

Covered in a film of lovemaking sweat, I left the vixen's chamber, pausing a moment to make sure the corridor was clear. Only two torches were lit, one at each end of the long passageway, leaving the middle to dim shadows, as I preferred.

Ballocks! A shadowy figure disappeared round a corner.

A spy. I must have missed him slinking against the wall.

After just having told Emma we needed to be more careful, I should have gone back through my own room to leave. But her body was like an opiate, leaving me in a euphoric state, and obviously with my defenses down. I had to be more careful. There was no time to ponder it. Guard back up, I made chase.

"Halt!" I shouted, the boom of my voice bouncing off the stone walls.

The hurried footsteps only grew faster, clattering as they scrabbled to make haste. Blood pumped fast through my veins as I hurried my pace. If the maggot wanted a chase, he'd get one. I wasn't going to back down. As I ran, I pictured the intruder in my mind—a head shorter than myself, covered in a black cloak. Could have been a woman, but more likely a man with the way the spy had run. A rugged, jerky gait, like that of hunted prey. How much had he heard? Her moans, my growls? Our declarations?

The wood of the door was thick, and I'd made an effort to swallow our cries of pleasure with kisses, but there was no telling if the stranger had knelt to the ground, his ear pressed to the crack beneath where our voices were much better carried through.

I gritted my teeth. Hating that there would never be any peace for Emma and I. That the stolen moments alone were all we were likely to get. Down the spiral stairs I went, taking them two at a time. I could hear the bastard's labored breath as I drew closer. He might be used to sneaking, but he wasn't used to running. The stairs were slippery, the centers worn into polished stone from years of use. Only a seasoned warrior would know how to step to avoid falling.

"I'll have your head," I growled, hoping to scare him into tripping. From the sound of flesh slapping stone, I believed I succeeded.

I practically leapt down the stairs. Almost on him. A swath of fabric flicked back to touch my feet as he rounded the spiral just ahead of me. I reached out to grab him. Just a few more inches and I'd be on him. Three more steps—

I came to a halt. Three servants knelt at the bottom of the stairs, scrubbing the stones and floorboards—two young boys and an older woman, mouths open.

No spy in sight. They glanced up at me wide-eyed. The two boys looked ready to piss themselves, but the woman simply pointed at the door conveniently leading outside.

"Damn," I muttered. I stepped over the boys and pushed the door. It was stuck. I growled and heaved, shoved my shoulder using all the strength within me. It budged a couple of inches.

The bastard had put something in front of the door to block me. He was likely long gone, but I wasn't going to let that deter me. There was no way in hell I was going to let him get away.

I took a wide step back and kicked the heel of my boot above the handle. The door splintered, obliterated beneath my foot. I shoved my way through the broken boards, into the mid-morning sun streaming down onto the dirt-packed courtyard, a few clan members gaped, their expressions startled. A dog who'd been wolfing down a leg of foul scampered away, crows pressing in on his abandoned treat.

"Where?" I growled to those present.

All of them lifted their arms to point toward the stables. The doors were closed. There was no one outside the building. He must have slipped inside. I nodded to the startled clansmen and stalked toward the stables. There was nowhere to run now. He was trapped.

A grin spread over my lips. I liked being the victor. And I was going to make the witless sac pay for his mistakes — and pay publicly. Had to send a message to those who would follow in his footsteps. Traitors would not be tolerated. Disloyalty would be punished severely.

I paused outside the stables, listening for any sounds inside. The usual nicker of horses, a hound growling somewhere beyond, and voices. More than one voice. They spoke hurriedly, as though in panic.

More than one traitor? 'Haps one who directed the maggot to listen outside Emma's door?

I banged open the door, chest puffed, taking up the entrance in a manner I knew would provoke fear. The door clattered against the wall and several horses whinnied loudly, the sound piercing. The scents of hay, horses and leather wafted out.

Three lads in poorly kept plaids stood in the center, their hushed whispers ceased as they whipped their heads around to face me. Eyes wide and startled. I vaguely recognized them. They weren't the lads usually in charge of the horses. The hair on the back of my neck raised on end. Normally, I would have told myself to remain calm, but being that a spy had led me to this very spot, I couldna let my instincts be pushed aside. Something wasn't right.

"M—my laird," one finally managed. His brown hair was greasy, his face covered in pock marks and he had deep pockets of purple beneath his eyes. He shivered, and swiped tendrils from his forehead.

"Who?" I growled, realizing I'd only been speaking in single syllables since chasing the traitor. I took an imposing step forward. "Tell me who he is and where he is. Now."

"My laird?" The taller of the three spoke, a subtle shift in his spine as he straightened it.

I stared at him, my face void of emotion, daring him to continue. Was the lad actually trying to challenge me, or only to not shite himself?

"Were my words unclear?" I said, low, menacing.

The taller lad quickly shook his head, his shoulders rounding slightly. His face took on a hint of green. I would have retreated a pace to keep him from vomiting on me, but the way he swallowed repeatedly showed that at least he had some sense to keep it in.

I stepped forward, noting that though their feet didn't move, the lads inched away all the same, leaning far enough back I thought they'd lose their balance. I had a keen urge to blow out a breath just to see them topple. "Then answer the fucking question."

"I—he—we—"

'Twas a miracle I kept from rolling my eyes and lashing out. The blasted lad had forgotten his tongue.

A deafening crash reverberated through the courtyard and into the stables. "What in bloody hell?"

Bloody fucking timing. I stepped back outside, trying to decipher where the boom came from. Were we under attack? I saw no enemies, no warriors running. Had an outbuilding collapsed? None looked to be out of place. The guards atop the battlements pointed, shouted toward the keep and out at the fields beyond. They didn't raise an alarm, however. I glowered and glanced toward the castle where voices were raised and people ran. Small stones crumbled down the side of the wall, and I could see that a large sized hole gaped somewhere around the second floor. We'd been hit by something. Looked to be the work of a large stone, flung from a trebuchet. But how was that possible?

The spy would have to wait.

"Don't move, or I'll cut off your ballocks and feed 'em to the hounds," I ordered the tongue-tied trio, before running back toward the keep where people had gathered in a wide circle.

They parted in a line as I walked forward, bowing their heads to me. Being the Guardian of Scotland, Laird of Gealach was good. I had power, I had the respect of my people. But what I didna have was what truly belonged to me, what had been stolen. For so long, I'd thought I didna want it. That what had been taken from me was a blessing in disguise. But I had to wonder, if my fate had been dealt differently—would I have so many enemies clambering at my door, or would the entire country bow to my feet? Would I be a good king?

As the crowd parted, a stone as large as a calf sat cracked in the middle three feet from the base of the keep. Other than the hole, no other damage had been done.

"Is anyone hurt?" I called out to the crowd. Everyone shook their head. "Inside?" I glanced toward the steps of the keep where the housekeeper shook her head. Thank God no one was injured.

This was an act of war. I turned to my men atop the battlements. "Report!" I bellowed.

A guard leapt from where he stood, sliding his way down the stairs and running toward me.

"My laird." He bowed. "I am glad to report we are not under attack."

"Not? What do ye mean? Someone has attacked us." I wrenched my arm toward the offending stone, pointing out the obvious.

"Aye, my laird, but only with the single stone."

My fists curled, ready to pummel the idiot into the ground. "A single stone is only the first of it."

The man nodded eagerly, but didn't say anything further.

I gritted my teeth, fists burning to slam into his gut. "Where did it come from?"

"The trebuchet."

A bloody fucking giant rock slinging machine that no one noticed before it was used against us? Laughable. "What trebuchet?" Each syllable was clipped as I forced myself to speak slowly so as not to completely lose my temper.

"I will show ye, my laird."

I grunted, turned to stare at the stone, noting what looked like a piece of parchment sticking from beneath it. I knelt down, rolled the stone enough to grip the parchment and pull it free. A tar concoction had been used to attach it to the stone. Scrawled in black ink, it said, *Beware the dark. Beware thy enemies. No man, woman or child will be spared. They will all pay for your sins.* Below the written words was a drawing of an armored fist — MacDonald's seal.

A threat. And not a veiled one.

I rolled the parchment and tucked it into the sporran at my hip. No one need see the threats of our enemy. No one need fear more than they already did.

I ignored the direct questions of my people, simply saying, "'Tis all right. Go back about your business. Be on alert for anything unusual. Come and tell me immediately if you see something, or have information regarding this incident. You are safe here." I pointed at several of the men. "Get these stones cleaned up inside and out. Find the clan mason and have him prepare a mortar to begin repairing the wall."

I followed the guard back to the battlements, climbing the stairs two at a time. When we reached the top he pointed out over the marsh, where trees dotted up against the mountainside.

"The trebuchet is there, my laird."

Centered in front of the trees was a single, crudely built, trebuchet.

I gritted my teeth so hard I felt the veins pop from my neck. Had all the men drunk from the same moron cask this morning? "'Tis obvious, why did no one see it approach?"

The men shifted uncomfortably. "We didna see it, my laird."

"How the hell did ye nay see it?" I shouted, anger coursing through my veins. Temper be damned. "'Tis a massive piece of fucking machinery!"

God save them, the men blushed.

"My laird, they played a trick on us."

"Trick?" I let out a breath slowly, trying not to beat them into a bloody pulp. I was so incensed, 'twas bound to happen within seconds.

"The trees, ye see?"

Glancing at the spot, I could see that it did look as though a few trees had been displaced, their branches on the ground behind the trebuchet.

"What is your guess, lads, and dinna skirt around your words any longer. Did they disguise the trebuchet? Did it magically appear from their arses?"

The men swallowed, all knowing where this was leading. I was about one sword-width away from pummeling the next man to speak.

"My laird." The voice of Ewan, my second, my most trusted clan warrior, spoke from behind me. "I think I know."

I turned around, to see Ewan holding one of my warriors, shackled. Augustus. Named after a Roman. We should have known not to trust him.

"Tell me," I said.

"They did nay disguise it, nor fart it out," Ewan said the latter with a smile. "Augustus is our scout on the north side. He simply allowed them to build it beyond the trees, and push it forward when the time came."

I took a step toward the traitor, yet another one. His breath was stale, and eyes bloodshot, puffy from being punched, no doubt by Ewan himself. Hints of bruising already pulled to the surface.

"How many others?" I asked in a low, calm tone.

Augustus swallowed, his lip split and bleeding. "Just that one."

"I dinna believe ye." If he'd allowed one to be built, there were more. And it wasn't only to send me a threatening message.

"Why?" A simple question put, but one that proved to be too complicated.

Augustus searched my eyes, his own filled with fear. He didna blurt out that he'd been forced. Didna say he'd not noticed it. The truth stared me in the face. He was a traitor.

"Strip him, tie him and give him a hundred lashes with the angry cat."

He'd be lucky to live through the first half. The angry cat was a cat-o-nine tails I saved for traitors. It had nine long corded leather plaits woven around wire and tipped with stones. 'Twas not meant for a man to live and I'd only had to use it one other time. Sourness built in the pit of my stomach.

"My laird," the man screeched. "Please! I beg ye, I know I've done ye wrong, and I swear to ye, I'll never do so again."

"This I know," I said, tone dull. It never did anyone good to beg for their lives, especially when they'd put the entire clan in danger.

He was lucky that no one was injured by the hurtling stone, else his punishment would have been worse by tenfold. The angry cat wasn't the only punishing weapon in our dungeon.

My stomach knotted and pain seared across my forehead. I was angry, filled with a rage that made my insides burn, and yet, sadness, too. What caused Augustus to turn against us? To essentially lie in wait as his people, his leader, were murdered?

I had to turn away, had to push away that human part of me that wanted badly to listen to the man, to hear his plea and believe him to be sincere. But no man allowed a trebuchet to be built on his watch unless he wanted to see serious damage done. There was no remorse in that. I had hundreds of people to protect here at Gealach—thousands more in all of Scotland. A king to protect. A secret to guard.

Any warrior who allowed the enemy to lie in wait and gave them an advantage, was no friend of ours. And no man to be redeemed.

This could only end in his punishment. His death.

And a lesson to our people.

"Ewan, see it done."

CHAPTER THREE

Emma

Logan walked down the steps, his usual powerful stance slightly altered. He still stood tall, shoulders straight, muscles coiled. Power emanated from his body with each movement. A storm cloud covered his face, eyes dark and filled with turmoil, lips firmly pressed down. The only thing different was that instead of staring into the eyes of each person he passed, he looked straight ahead. Living inside his mind. He looked haunted.

I couldn't imagine what conversation had been had atop the castle walls. I'd seen Ewan drag the other warrior up the stairs and present him to Logan. Watched the play of anger and disgust cross over their laird's features. He was beyond rage. The warrior must have done something. Could even be the reason behind the loud crash heard a quarter hour earlier.

I'd been standing by the window, preparing, yet again, how I would tell Logan about myself. Psyching myself up for the feat of spilling such ludicrous news when the crash had happened. The sound vibrated the air, the walls shook, and I'd jumped, flailing my arms, ready for the entire castle to fall around me, burying us all in a crumbled, mortared mess.

But that hadn't happened. Instead, everything went still and then shouts came from outside. I watched everyone run toward the castle, saw the huge rock cracked on the ground. Logan burst from the stables, fury written on his face. Chills swept over me and made my knees shake. I gripped the casement just like I had earlier that morning while Logan and I were together but this time for an entirely different reason—it was helping me stand up.

While everyone else looked toward the castle, I gaped out at the field as four men ran as though their lives depended on it—going from the castle toward the forest. Their plaids were worn as their boots. They stumbled, one fell, but that didn't stop them. The others ran ahead while he scrambled to his feet, tripping all the more as he went. Within a minute, they were all behind the trees, and those who stood guard, appeared to have missed it entirely.

With a castle that always seemed to be under attack, I was more than surprised that such a divergence had been accomplished. No one looked toward the fields? Unbelievable. And what even happened? How did they get the giant rock over the wall? There appeared to be some sort of wooden contraption at the edge of the forest, but I couldn't truly see what it was. Looked almost like a giant sling-shot. But it was at the edge of the forest—which meant those four would not have been able to man it. They'd come from the inside.

Impossible. The guards would have seen it. The men would have had to climb over the wall. How could that have been missed, unless they climbed at the moment of impact, hoping to have escaped when no one was looking. But still…

Unless, more than a few were in on Logan's demise, not just the idiot who tore up my medieval lingerie. The man who Ewan brought was a guard, one of their own. He was in shackles. A traitor. It begged the question of how many of his guards were traitors.

I shuddered. I'd not left my room since the shorn fabric had been found. Kept imagining some psychopath, teeth bared and slick as they eagerly stabbed again and again at the flimsy material, probably wishing I was still inside it.

I wrung my hands, staring off at the empty grounds where the perpetrators had just run across. Watched atop the castle wall as Ewan dragged a screaming man down the stairs, and the guards still standing nodded after him. They agreed with whatever was about to happen to the man. I hated to think what it could be. Logan hadn't even looked that disturbed when he'd taken prisoners, or questioned MacDonald.

The man flailed, bellowed, begged, cried.

Ewan tied him to a post in the center of the courtyard. I'd not noticed it before, but when I thought back on it, it had been used for tying horses.

The man was pressed facing the post, his shirt cut entirely from his body. Kilt ripped away. He stood nude, skin quivering, not from cold, but had to be from fear.

"Get the angry cat," Ewan shouted to a man standing not five feet away.

He, too, sounded disturbed. What was the angry cat and why did they need it to punish this man? I imagined a hellish feline, being unleashed from its cage to wreak havoc on this poor soldier's back.

But I didn't imagine the wicked looking instrument that was presented to Ewan. A whip of sorts, but one that looked like a nightmare. Multiple cords with what appeared to be razors at its end. An involuntary shudder took hold. What sort of damage could be done with that monstrosity? Too much...

I stared wide-eyed, swallowing hard. Unable to move, my eyes riveted to a scene I didn't want to see. Like rubberneckers on the highway gawking at a horrible accident, I couldn't look away.

The man was going to be tortured.

I didn't doubt his crime was heinous. Didn't doubt that Logan was furious and felt righteous in his decision. Wouldn't question him for fear of angering him further.

But, Logan had looked haunted. Though he had to do this, I could tell he hadn't wanted to.

Sympathy for Ewan made my stomach turn with nausea. How could he stand being the one to implement such a punishment?

The first crack of that horrid whip screamed through the air, tearing into the warrior's back, only drowned by the sounds of the man's own screaming.

Blood and flesh flew from that one hit, and he'd not stopped his scream before Ewan wrenched back and lashed him again.

Red stripes covered his back and he'd only been hit twice.

I couldn't watch anymore. Closing the shutters, I turned from the scene, but even that didn't cut the sound from outside or the sights still burned into my eyes.

I sank to the floor, shaking, dizzy. The lashing whip and screams found their way through the cracks in the shutter, reaching my ears and tearing at my heart.

I couldn't stay here. Couldn't listen to it.

Leaping to my feet I rushed to my door and threw it open. The hallway was dark and empty, and with each step I took, the sounds of the man being tortured outside lessened. Cold, wet, tears tracked down my cheeks. I'd not even been aware that I was crying until the salt touched my lips. Down the hall I went, descending the stairs. Anytime the sound grew louder I turned away from it, until I found myself outside of Logan's office.

I lifted my hand to knock just as a slit in the center of the door opened and a sword thrust out. I screamed, jumped away, hitting my back against the wall behind me and stumbling forward. The door was thrown open and Logan reached for me, grasping me in his arms before I fell.

My heart beat so fast I was sure to faint.

"Oh, my God," he whispered, lips pressed to my hair, breath tickling my scalp. "*Mo creach*... I almost killed ye. What are ye doing here?"

He shook. Strong and powerful, Logan. He trembled with...fear?

"I'm all right," I whispered back, sliding my arms around his waist. I held on tight for purchase, hoping that with my own quivering body, I could still his tremble.

"Thank the saints." He pressed his face further into my hair, breathing heavily.

Power flowed between us. Emotion, deep and cutting. I let out a shuddering breath, realizing how close I'd come. The steel of his blade a few inches from slicing my belly.

The stark reality of where I was, and how little technology had developed hit deep. The doctors here were also cooks and Lord knew what else. I was more likely to die from the ministrations of such medical attention than from the wound itself. It seemed the likelihood of being attacked was multiplied by the hundreds compared to the twenty-first century. Was being with Logan worth dying for?

I pressed my face to his chest, nose flush to the muscles of his pectoral, breathed in his earthy, masculine scent. Maybe. Yes. God, it was a hard question to ask.

"Are ye sure ye're all right?" he asked. "That had to have scared the hell out of ye."

I nodded, massaging my fingers into his spine. "I'm fine."

"What were ye doing out here?" His hands splayed flat on my lower back, inching closer to the cushion of my buttocks.

"I was…running."

"From what?"

"The noise." Images of the warrior's raw, flayed back flashed. I closed my eyes, trying to get rid of them, but the blood only grew darker.

"From the stone? Were ye that scared, then? How long have ye been running or were ye lost?"

I shook my head, my lips brushing his shirt, skin starting to tingle. "No, I was running from the sound of the man being beaten."

"Och, I see," he said, low, regretfully. "That canna be helped. I'm sorry for ye to have heard it."

"I saw some of it."

Logan groaned, held me tighter. "Not a sight for a lass."

"A sight I saw nonetheless. Was it…" I hesitated, not wanting him to get angry with me for questioning him. We might be lovers, but that didn't mean that Logan didn't still hold himself—as he should—above me in his position within the clan. Outside the bedroom, we weren't equals. That was something that was likely never to change.

"Was it, what?" His tone was inviting, encouraging.

I sucked in a breath, readying myself to ask. "What did he do to deserve it?"

Logan lost some of his tension. Thank God. I'd been afraid, that even though he was inviting, he would have been irritated when I questioned him. "Ah, so ye want to know if 'twas necessary?"

I nodded, afraid my voice wouldn't work quite right.

"He is a traitor. Let our enemies build a trebuchet right beyond the trees in order to attack us with that stone."

Wow… That was pretty bad. But enough to die over? "Trebuchet… The sling shot thing?"

Logan eyed me oddly. "Sling shot?" He raised a brow as he always did when I said something off kilter.

"Never mind. Was there only the one? Isn't that odd? Was it not an attack, but a threat?"

"Aye, a threat."

"What is the threat?" My head reeled, trying to understand it all. "Did he have to die over it?"

"Ye wouldna understand. Ye were nay hurt by the stone, were ye?" Logan changed the subject.

He didn't want to tell me everything. I was used to that, but it still sent a prickle of irritation skating over my nerves. I should trust his decision. He was intelligent, had ruled his clan successfully, and since I'd been there, kept everyone safe despite numerous threats. But I was a woman. And in this era, women shouldn't ask questions. I tried not to frown and decided to play along, maybe that would help him in gaining trust enough to tell me something more.

"No. I did see something, though."

"What?" Logan pulled away, and I had to curl my fingers to keep from tugging him back.

"Four men running across the grass toward the trees."

"What trees?"

"Where the sling-shot—trebuchet—was."

"They were on foot?"

"Yes. I think they must have climbed over the walls from the courtyard. They were running like the devil was on their heels."

"And he likely was." Logan furrowed his brow, pursed his lips in thought. "If ye saw the bastards would ye be able to identify them."

"I think so. Do you think you can catch them?"

"Likely they are already caught."

I had my doubts about that. "I don't think the guards on the wall saw."

That made him frown all the more. This time when he tensed, I knew it wasn't fear driving him. Rage burned hot in his eyes, and for a moment, when his gaze swept over me I was afraid, until my sense kicked in. This man wasn't a danger to me. Not like Steven had been.

I trusted Logan. A trust he'd earned and continued to gain. While I didn't share every piece of myself with him, I wanted to, and that was a major step in my book.

"Why do ye say that, lass?"

I loved the way his words rolled off his tongue. Sensual. Dangerous.

"Because I was watching."

"What were ye watching?"

I met his gaze, held it, wanted him to see I spoke the truth. He sounded so skeptical, and I couldn't blame him. The man couldn't blink without being thwarted.

"I was just looking out the window, people watching —"

"People watching?"

A term he probably wasn't used to… One of those things, I always seemed to say things that hadn't yet been coined. "Yes, watching everyone." I shrugged, acting nonchalant. I wasn't going to tell him that I'd been rehearsing in my mind how to tell him my darkest secrets. But I wasn't a good liar either, and I was sure by the way he searched my face, some part of me was giving away that I wasn't telling the whole truth. "I was bored. And," I bit my lip for effect, "I was a little scared of leaving my room after you found my nightgown shredded." That *was* the truth.

"Och, lass." He pulled me against him again, enfolding me with his arms. He was hot, hard, and all I wanted to do was kiss him and forget what I'd heard, seen.

"Tell me more of what ye saw."

"I saw the men running over the field. I looked to the guards, sure they'd seen what I saw, but they only looked toward the castle, like everyone else."

"The men were running away from the castle when the rock hit?"

"Yes."

"Hmm." Logan didn't share his thoughts, but I could almost hear his mind turning, contemplating.

"That means there are more. If the men were running away, they couldn't have operated the trebuchet."

"Aye."

"Gosh, Logan..."

"Nay, lass, dinna fash over it. I'm still reeling from nearly killing ye." He ended the conversation there, pressing me hard up against the wall.

Every ridge, line and bulge demanding a response.

"Logan... Someone could see..." That seemed to be the theme of the day. Hot, powerful, out in the open sex.

Almost like our conversation early that morning about having to be more secretive was bringing about this new side where Logan wanted everyone to see us. To hear our passion and be a part of it.

I'd be lying if I said it was exhilarating, thrilling—like getting your first kiss on the front porch, hoping your parents didn't open the door to see your hot crush's tongue down your throat. Or notice that your nipples were hard as diamonds, and eyes glazed like a sugary doughnut.

In one fell swoop, he tossed me over his shoulder, and took me back into his library, slamming the door behind us, the lock clicking as he turned the key in place. I laughed, and slapped him playfully on the back.

"Put me down," I said.

"Problem solved, aye?" He rubbed his hand over my ass and then set me down on the edge of his desk.

"Aye," I murmured, imitating his brogue—a sound I still couldn't get over.

"I've never had a woman in here." His breath tickled my neck as he skimmed his lips along its length.

"I'm the first?

He nodded, his whiskered chin bumping against my neck, rasping, tantalizing. Logan ran his tongue up the column, ending at the lobe of my ear. "And most likely the last."

My breath lodged in my throat. Had he really just said that? What did it mean? But before my thoughts could get away from me, Logan's mouth covered mine, and he roughly yanked my gown up over my legs.

His fingers dug into my thighs as he wrenched them apart. He was rough, but I found I liked it. Wanted to be taken by him like this. I slid my arms around his waist, and gripped his ass, tugging him closer. When his fingers slid along my inner thigh, then dipped into my drenched sex, I moaned, my body coming alive.

"Christ, lass," Logan growled against my lips.

Things moved fast from there, urgent, intense. Logan tugged at his belt, his plaid falling with a soft thud to the floor. The length of his hard cock bobbed against my inner thigh, but before I could reach between us to grip it, he lifted my hips and surged forward.

His kiss swallowed my cry of pleasure, but didn't lessen the scratch of nails against his back. Dear God, he was massive. Powerful. And had all the right moves. He pumped in and out of me, swiveled his hips. Reached between our bodies and stroked my clit until I could no longer breathe. Within seconds I felt like I would break apart with pleasure, and he only pounded into me harder.

The wooden legs of the desk scraped over the floorboards, rattling and echoing in the room. Our skin slapped feverishly, and still he kissed me, his tongue sliding relentlessly against mine. I kissed him back with such ferocity, I wanted to swallow him whole.

Orgasm struck — like lightning. I bucked against him, back arching, moaning into his kiss. Logan growled, nipping at my lower lip as he pushed forward harder, faster, and then I felt the hot spurt of his finish. He shook beneath my thighs, the muscles of his ass tightening beneath my fingertips.

This was a quick, pleasure seeking moment. Not the lessons he normally gave, but the two of us needing release. Needing to bathe in each other's essence in order to forget the happenings of the day.

God, how I loved him.

CHAPTER FOUR

Emma

Logan escorted me back to my room, limp and sated. I wanted to stretch out on my bed like a lazy cat and stare up at the ceiling, waiting until the next time we'd see each other. I was giddy, excited and nervous at the same time. With all the craziness of today, that was bound to be hours and hours away.

The heat of his fingers coiled around my arm sent shivers racing over my already tingling skin. The halls were dim and nearly empty, a stray servant scurrying out of their laird's path every so often as they went about their chores.

It was only when we reached my door, and I stared at the old wood, scratched and worn from age, iron black and so very medieval, that the euphoria of our lovemaking dissipated. "What will you do now?" I glanced down at the ground, half expecting to see something torn up again. But the floor was clear outside my door just as it was outside Logan's.

"Make sure your chamber is safe."

I smiled, wondering if I might entice him to stay for round two, a distraction I desperately needed as the beaten warrior's cries echoed off the stone walls. But I wasn't feeling gutsy enough to say it.

He opened the door and looked from side to side. It was just as I'd left it, the shutters closed. Thank goodness the only sounds from outside were those of the men working on the repairing the walls. I could hear the clink of a hammer or chisel against stone, and calls for mortar and other things.

Logan looked inside my wardrobe, beneath the bed, behind the tapestries. I smiled at his diligence in keeping me safe.

"Empty," he said, sounding mildly surprised.

"Were you expecting me to have a guest?" I asked, a teasing brow raised.

Logan curled one side of his lip up in a smile. "'Haps an unwanted one."

I sauntered forward, put my hands behind my back to keep from reaching out and touching him. I knew he had to go. Had things to do. A castle to take care of, a secret threat to diffuse. Was it selfish of me to want him all for myself? I knew the answer to that. Didn't have to ask it.

Yes. I couldn't. He couldn't.

Damn, but his era was so much harder than my own.

Then again—life for me in the twenty-first century had not been very pleasant. So many days filled with terror. Years passed with me walking on eggshells. Not anyway for someone to live. I barely existed, a shadow of a human being, breathing only to see to my husband's pleasure and keep his anger at bay.

"You're the only guest I want," I said, connecting my eyes with his. I was serious. It wasn't a ploy to have him pick me up and toss me onto the bed. I wanted him to know that he truly was the one person who mattered to me—words I wasn't brave enough to utter.

A cloud spread over Logan's face, and he glanced away. I stopped dead in my tracks, unsure of what that could mean. He was so closed off with his emotions, it was hard to tell what he felt at any given moment. In the throes of passion, he would call out to me, tell me how much he needed me, how I healed him, made him whole. But when we weren't physically connected, there was an emotional disconnect.

Was the only way to gain insight into his thoughts when his body was inside mine?

Before I could stop myself, I asked, "What is it?"

Logan smiled, his gaze sliding back to mine. "When ye first came to Gealach, ye'd not have asked me what I was thinking."

"Is it wrong to ask?" I stopped myself from saying I would do anything he asked of me.

"Nay, lass." He stepped closer but didn't touch me.

His nearness tortured me. I could feel the heat of him, smell him.

I bit my lip, contemplating if I would ask him more. Time to bite the bullet—or sword. "Logan, what's bothering you? You know you can tell me anything."

That shield-cloud came over his features again. I wanted to groan, to stomp my foot and demand he share something with me. To point out how much I'd given up by being not only at his castle, but in this room.

And I was grateful to be here. Not just for the amazing sex, the comfort of his embrace, and the healing that he created in my soul, but because I couldn't imagine walking around in that horrid wilderness where men feasted on the flesh of those weaker than they. I didn't want to live that way. Not before I came here and certainly not now.

I'd escaped one kind of hell for another—but each was completely different. In my own time, my personal life was hell, and outside the door to my house, the grass was always greener in my neighbor's lawn. In this world, my personal life was heaven, and outside the door, danger lurked—my life was not even guaranteed.

A notion that made choosing between the two times harder still. I could change my personal life anywhere, but the outside world was a different story.

That's when it came down to how Logan marked my soul, my heart. I couldn't live without him.

Danger or not, I wanted to stay with him. But he had to know the risks, too. And he had to be willing to open up to me.

I pushed forward a little, pressing my palm to his chest.

"Open up to me," I whispered.

He glanced down at my hand pressed to his shirt.

"I want to," he said, lifting his gaze back up to mine.

"But you can't. Or you won't."

Regret played on his features. "'Tis a little bit of both, lass."

Circles. I felt like we were running around in a never ending circle. The heat of annoyance burned in my stomach. I was the first woman he'd made love to in his office. The words he whispered to me, the way he'd been so frightened when he nearly killed me. All these things pointed to something so much more meaningful and deep. And yet, he refused to open up to me. In fact, was pushing me away.

"One day, you'll have to open up to me. We can't just keep going on like this." I purposefully kept my words soft, not wanting them to be said in anger.

"And have ye told me everything? Have ye opened up all the way?" He had me there. How easily he could read me.

I bit my lip. There was no reason to lie. I hadn't told him everything, even when I'd wanted to. Now didn't seem like the right time. "Seems we both need to be more forthcoming."

"Aye. 'Twould appear that way." The muscle in the sides of his jaw ticked.

"I feel safest when I'm with you," I said, hoping that would appease him somewhat. It was the truth, and one I'd not told him. I did feel safe with him. Like everything would be fine and the nightmare's melted away.

Logan's expression didn't change, and I had no clue what was going on inside his mind. "Is that a confession?"

I shrugged, nodded. It certainly felt like one. I searched his face, his eyes, but they gave no clues to his thoughts. "I've never felt so safe in my life. Even with all…the stuff going on in your world."

"My world? Is it nay your world, too?" He raised a questioning brow.

I swallowed hard. I'd made a mistake. A slip of the tongue. I cocked my head, trying for coy. "I was hoping it would be." The seductive curl I added to my lips seemed to do the trick as his eyes roved there.

I'd never tried to play that game before. Never been that kind of girl. Didn't believe I could pull it off. But I did. Like I was some sort of sex kitten for a minute. It felt good. Freeing. Powerful.

What was it about this place, this man, that set me free?

It also was the perfect distraction away from confessing that we both had secrets to tell, and neither of us had been forthcoming.

"'Tis already." He gripped the side of my hip and pulled me flush against him. "I'd have the world know it, if it were nay for the bastards tearing up your enticing gowns."

That acknowledgment made me smile. When he said things like that, I caught a glimpse of the man inside, the things he wanted.

I stared up at him, at the creases at the ends of his eyes, the firm line of his mouth—knowing all the sensual things he could do with those lips—the sharp edge to his jaw. He was rugged, hard, and yet he made me melt. Logan was beautiful.

He bent low over me, his breath tickling across my chin. Lips pressed roughly to mine, demanding I surrender, and I did—wholly. I sagged against him, clutched at the front of his shirt. Logan sank his tongue into my mouth, velvet soft and intense. I leaned up into him, rubbing myself pelvis to his, my breasts to his chest, wanting desperately for him to take me to bed. But instead, he pulled away, pushed me back. His face was as stricken as I felt. A chill washed over me.

"Ye might be the death of me," he said low. Not a whisper, but a gruff exhale. He didn't look at me, but instead trained his gaze to the left side of me, as though just looking at me might send him hurling from the window.

And then he left. Walked out of the room without a backward glance, or a goodbye. Simply vanished, leaving me staring after the space where he'd once stood.

Pressing a hand to my belly, I worked to calm my uneven breaths. He opened up one second, and shut down the next. Made my heart do flips, my sex clench so tight I was on the verge of orgasm every minute of the day. And just like that he walked away. Left me high and dry. As though he weren't attached—or was afraid to admit it. It was embarrassing, devastating.

I suddenly felt like the walls were caving in around me. I had to get out of this room. I'd spent so much of my time in the present locked up, caged. I wasn't going to do that here. Hadn't I vowed that the old Mrs. Gordon was gone? That this new, adventurous Emma was here to stay? I couldn't shrink back into that woman now. Though, it was a safety net, a protective mode, I had to overcome it.

There were no edicts here on who I could and couldn't be. Logan wanted me for who I was, and I was still learning who that person was. Hiding wasn't going to help me figure that out at all.

Straightening my shoulders, I headed toward the door. A little twinge of disappointment hit when I didn't see Logan in the hallway. I suppose part of me wanted him to come back. To admit that he was afraid to tell me his secrets and the secrets of his castle. He'd beg for my forgiveness, sweep me into his arms and confess everything I wanted to know.

I almost laughed aloud. That was so completely not Logan. He might sweep me off my feet, but he didn't confess, he growled, and I doubted he'd ever told anyone anything about himself. He was closed off. Had his own moat, a thick stone wall, portcullis and army of imaginary guards to hide his heart.

The quiet of the castle made the hair on the back of my neck stand on end. It was dark, still, the kind of place that allowed demons to form from shadows and the Boogie Man to leap out from behind every corner. I forged on, even though my hands trembled. At some point, I would get used to the creep factor. I had to.

I made my way down the winding stairs, through another hallway and then opened the door that led to the great hall — sure to avoid the booby-trapped door of Logan's office. I waited for a servant to ask what I needed, or to glare me from the room, but it was empty. This morning's whipping seemed to make the whole of the clan disappear. No doubt, they were all keeping a low profile in case the laird chose to make an example of someone else. But didn't they understand that the man who was beaten today had been a traitor? Their laird wasn't a vicious, cruel man. He did what he thought was right and just. And it just so happened that in this place, what was right and just for a traitor was death.

Maybe they were all traitors.

I couldn't think on that. It was too diabolical. I headed straight for the grand tapestry that hid the secret door. The woven colors vibrant. The king giving a sacred gift to the knight who knelt before him. I'd once thought it to be Logan, though he didn't look much like him. Logan corrected me — the man was his father.

The gift was the secret of Gealach, and I meant to find out what it was. I hoped that it would help me to figure out Logan. To understand him better. Assuage the fact that he would tell me I'd be the death of him and then disappear.

If he died… I couldn't even think about it. Even those three simple words flitting through my mind made me want to run screaming from myself.

I shook my head and slipped behind the tapestry. The wall looked the same, no evidence of a hidden door, but I knew where it was. The last time I'd come in here, I'd been in the dark, and been too nervous to explore. Things had changed now, and I was finally willing to enter the darkened cavern.

A shiver stole over me. But not without light.

I slipped out from behind the tapestry and glanced around the great hall. Atop the mantle of the fireplace was a smaller candelabra—four candles, burned halfway down. Beside it looked like a tinder box—a flint inside for lighting flames.

How did a flint work? I didn't know. But I had watched Logan and the maids use it to light candles and fires. Looked easy enough. If the candles blew out, then I could relight them.

With another glance around to make sure I was alone, I grabbed the flint, stuffed it into the bodice of my gown and picked up the candelabra. My heart beat erratically, fingers trembled. I was going to lose my nerve.

Shit.

I couldn't go through with it!

I knew for certain there was something down those stairs. Something secretive that Logan, maybe even the whole of the clan, didn't want me to know. A secret. A treasure. Maybe the very box depicted in that gorgeous tapestry.

But I was frightened of the dark. I stared into the candle flames, glowing orange and yellow. They barely flickered, except for with each exhalation of my breath.

I had to do this. I'd been putting it off for weeks, months.

Now. Before anyone found me standing there with the candelabra and a tinder box stuffed down my front. That would be hard to explain.

I ran across the room, my footsteps echoing loudly on the floor. Booming. I expected everyone to come running to find out what I was about to do. I stopped behind the tapestry, feeling closed off from the world. No one came. No one noticed. Again I found myself staring into the flames. I blew out two of the candles to conserve them.

With a deep breath, I felt along the stones of the wall, pressing gently until I found that one stone that caved in slightly and silently. I pushed harder, my heart leaping into my throat as it sunk into the wall several inches. Now or never.

I probed the inside of the crevice, dust and crumbled rock meeting my fingertips. And then, there it was, my finger caught on the same iron hook from months before. I tugged, biting my lip and waiting to hear a loud creaking sound. Waited for the great hall to erupt with noise.

Nothing.

Again, just a soundless whoosh of air, as the door swept open a few inches. Darkness beckoned and warned at the same time.

My heart skipped a beat. How could it be so easy?

What I was about to do would change everything. But I was willing to do it.

I stepped through the doorway. Complete blackness lit by the glow of my candles, but only ten feet or so in front of me, before meeting the darkness again.

I slid my feet forward, as though my body refused to let me go through with what I wanted. Down one step.

Then I realized, I had to shut the door. I turned, ready to close it, when the false panel closed of its own accord. The sudden shift in the air blew out the candles, leaving me consumed by darkness.

CHAPTER FIVE

Logan

The only sound greater than the rush of rage-filled blood pounding through my ears was the clash of my boot heels against the floorboards as I paced the length of my study.

Bloody fucking hell.

The MacDonald was worse than a dull thorn shoved deep in my arse. The man was a fool. A stubborn fool. If only I'd disobeyed my brother, the king. Killed MacDonald when I had a chance and made my apologies later. James could punish me if he had the will to do so. For certes, he wouldna be thanking me, though he should.

Self-proclaimed leader of the Isles, MacDonald would one day be the doom of all Scots—Highlanders and Lowlanders alike, I had no doubt. There was no other future I could see. There would be no peaceful ending. The man would not bow out lightly. He was as rabid as they came, and he wanted me dead and my brother dethroned. There was nothing he wouldna do to get it, either. I was positive of that.

And now he'd infiltrated my men.

Dug right into the heart of Gealach and twisted his serrated blade. Anger sliced through me, hot and cold. Without thinking, I whirled on the stone wall behind me, bellowed my frustration and slammed my fist into the craggy surface. I shook the pain that radiated through my arm away.

How many others? I knew without a doubt there had nay been just one. The men in the stables—all a ruse. And one I'd fell for. Distracted by Emma—constantly.

Fucking her was a mistake. A grave one. For now I craved her like a starving man yearned for a crust of bread.

I couldna be taken for a fool again.

From hence forth, I would punish first, and take confessions later—if there was a later. I could no longer allow my enemies to walk among us.

The clan would learn quickly. A few examples would have to be made—all of which started with the lashing of the guard. I wondered if the fellow had survived his punishment or if he'd succumbed quickly, and I was dreadfully troubled that Emma had witnessed it.

Dammit. There she was again, invading my mind. I needed a drink.

The scrape of the door sounded at my back. Before the wood was full ajar, my sword was in hand, steel tip at Ewan's neck.

"Ballocks, give me warning," I grumbled, sheathing the sword. The second time I'd nearly killed someone close to me in one day.

"I might say the same," Ewan said, no hesitation in his tone.

That only soured my mood all the more. I trusted Ewan with my life. More so than anyone else in the clan. I could berate him for treating me like we were equals, but in truth, Ewan was a dose of reality in a world that seemed to always be fraught with nightmares.

"What do ye want?" The sharpness in my voice grabbed my second-in-command's attention.

He straightened, face grew slack and he said, "I thought ye might like to discuss the events of this afternoon."

I'd rather punch my own eyes out. But that would only leave me blind, and I had enough challenge seeing the lies of the world as it was. 'Haps this was why my right had been stripped from me. A fortune-teller had prophesied I would be inadequate.

"Aye." I walked over to the window, realizing as I went that my hand stung. I glanced down, noting the blood trickling from the split in my knuckles.

Punching stone had been an idiotic move. I flexed my hand, luckily able to move it. 'Twouldn't do to have broken a bone in my hand. I'd seen men removed from power for lesser reasons than that. Easily trumped by a man with the use of all his power. I grunted. Even with a broken hand, or anything else for that matter, I'd not let anyone get the better of me. Let them try. I dared them.

"Tell me of Augustus." I rubbed the blood from my knuckles with the end of my plaid.

"Made it to a dozen before he slumped full against the post. Thirty-six before his first loss of consciousness. Woke screaming at forty-nine. Eighty-seven before he went to the devil." Ewan's voice was grave. He despised meting out the punishments. Kept count of every last stroke. 'Twas the reason I mostly doled them out, but this time… I'd been too shaken by how my the carefully constructed defenses of the castle were being unraveled by our enemies.

I nodded sharply. "Devil held on longer than some."

"Aye, my laird. He cursed your name for all to hear."

"And?"

"Not a one called back to him, save to say he deserved the cat upon his back."

"Good." Wouldna help to have others agreeing. Outside the sun was starting to sink on the horizon, melting into the trees. Blood sprayed the ground near the whipping post and crows littered the area, pecking at the reddened ground. "The MacDonald has vowed his revenge." I walked over to the sideboard and poured Ewan and myself a dram. I didn't even have to convince him. He grabbed the cup and swigged it, holding it out for another before I'd finished mine.

I didn't blame him. He'd had to take a life in a most violent manner. 'Twas different than in battle. Though Augustus was an enemy, he was incapacitated when tied to the post. Made the whole business of it that much harder.

I guzzled the rest of mine and poured us both a healthier portion, the amber liquid sloshing over the side. Ewan swigged it back, gritting his teeth at the end.

"Burns nice, doesna it?"

"Aye, my laird."

I half-grinned and nodded. Whiskey took the edge off of everything. I poured a little over the cuts on my knuckles, hissing at the sting.

"Tell me of MacDonald," Ewan said, setting his mug down and putting his hands behind his back, standing at attention.

"Ye dinna have to stand there. I'm nay going to give ye orders just now. Sit." I pointed to one of the chairs surrounding the table I used to write letters, map out my holdings and the surrounding area.

Ewan nodded. "My thanks." He pulled out a chair and slumped into it. Blood was splattered on his fingers.

I picked up the basin of water on the table beside my bed and set it in front of him. "Wash the grime from your hands."

Ewan dipped his hands into the water, scrubbing away the blood of the traitor among us.

"A piece of parchment was attached to the stone," I began. "Beware the dark. Beware thy enemies. No man, woman or child will be spared. They will all pay for your sins. His seal was on it."

Ewan frowned and dried his hands on the towel I handed him. "The bastard wants us to come after him. He wants to start a bloody war."

"That thought crossed my mind." More than once. More than just now.

"He wants ye to leave the walls of Gealach. Ye'll be vulnerable if ye do. And so will the clan."

"Aye."

"But if ye stay, he'll believe ye fear him and he'll make the people believe ye fear him."

"Aye." The bastard truly had me by the ballocks.

"What will ye do?"

"Prepare a deception." MacDonald wanted me to be vulnerable. He wanted me to leave so he could more easily take over Gealach. Wanted to undermine my authority with the people. Times were scary as it was for the clan. If they believed I was too afraid to protect them…

"The people willna believe ye are afraid of MacDonald."

"At first," I said. "But soon, reason will disappear and doubt will take control of their sense. Suspicion will consume them." Brought to mind a term Emma used when we visited the clan sheep and she compared their pack behavior to humans using the servants as an example. Some of the sheep might run headlong toward the wolf.

"I'm nay certain I understand," Ewan said. His eyes were bloodshot, and he looked ready to pass into a deep sleep.

"The clan will side with me. They'll side with ye. Believe in what they see and remember—that I take care of them, keep them safe, have the ear of the king. But soon, rumors will fly. Doubt will creep beneath the surface of their skin, and they'll start to itch. Everything they see, hear, will be misconstrued. They'll question their beliefs, their memories. And then, they will question me. Doubt me. MacDonald's plan will work. Unless I divert him."

"With your deception."

"Aye." I pulled the knife from my boot and trailed it over the map unfolded on my table. "'Twill help us discover more conspirators."

"A rumor of your own?"

"Aye. Let us begin to tell a select few that we are preparing for war. That we will meet MacDonald on his own grounds. Tell some we're taking the ships north. Tell others we'll find him on foot—that we believe he's already here, surrounding us. Let us find out what comes back to us. We will know to a degree who can keep their mouth shut and who canna." I frowned down at the map, imagining each craig, marsh, glen and ravine in my mind. I stabbed the knife into the map. "Seems my choice to send him home in his shackles only fueled his hunger for revenge."

"Aye, my laird. But ye will beat him. Ye always do."

"This time I'll nay let him leave alive."

"And ye'll nay let him die quickly."

I shook my head, yanked the blade from the map and glowered. 'Twas time I spoke once more with MacDonald's cousin who resided, most uncomfortably, in my dungeon. "I need to question a prisoner. Ye go get some rest. We're bound to lose sleep in the coming days. When ye wake, we'll begin interviewing our men to see who is loyal and who is not."

Ewan followed me out and I locked the door behind us. He grumbled something before walking toward the stairs leading to the barracks and his sleeping quarters—a separate, small chamber off the hall where the men slept.

The guards stood aside when I reached the grated door to the dungeon, and into the darkness I slipped. Allan 'o the Wisp was separated from the rest of the prisoners, who were chained to a wall in one cell. MacDonald's vicious cousin Allan was known for his brutal ways. Setting fires to cottages and plundering women in every village he passed through. I was glad to have captured him not just for being my enemy's kin, but for his vile ways. The man would rot in prison until the king gave me permission to execute him.

Though it was dark, Allan must have sensed that I was there. "I wondered when ye'd come." His voice was raspy, and I could hear the sound of the iron shackles scrape as he moved.

I lit a torch on the wall beside his cell. He stood slowly, his body weakened from shortage of food and water. We weren't starving him, but we weren't giving him a daily feast either. Lack of movement would make his muscle cramp, and judging from the wince on his face, that was the case. Good. A weakened, uncomfortable man was less likely to succeed in escape. But all the same, I didna trust Allan 'o the Wisp.

"Tell me how many men within my army MacDonald has manipulated. Tell me what tasks they were charged with."

Allan chuckled, showing brown, rotting teeth, just as dirty as the rest of him had become. Obviously, he knew exactly what—or whom—I was talking about. "Och, Grant, ye canna expect me to tell ye nothing."

"On the contrary. I expect ye will."

"Then ye'll be waiting a long time."

Allan was a stubborn bastard. Loyal to a fault to his bastard cousin. Probably promised riches, or maybe even the hand of the lass who'd had him thrown off a cliff. Lucky for the bastard that he'd landed on a ledge and begged his way up. The lady and her guards should have let the devil rot.

"What can ye hope to gain?" I asked, pulling my dirk from my boot and cleaning my nails. I watched him carefully through lowered lids, pretending attention on my nails in hopes he'd give something away with his expression. "Ye'll rot within these walls. MacDonald willna be able to give ye what he promised."

Allan shrugged, his shoulder bones jutting up through the linen of his once white shirt. "'Haps he promised me nothing. 'Haps I just like to see ye suffer."

I peeled my lips back in a vicious smile and glanced up, making sure our eyes locked. "That's the thing, Allan, I'm nay suffering. But 'tis my duty, and my greatest desire, to peel the skin off those who defy the king. And it just so happens ye know whose skin I'm looking for. Whether ye tell me or not, doesna matter. I'll find out one way or another. But if ye tell me, I'll see ye eat well the rest of your days in that cell."

Allan licked his lips and I swore I heard his stomach growl. Probably imagined a big, juicy leg of fowl, grease slithering over his tongue and succulent meat melting in his mouth. 'Twas enough for some men to give up on what they believed in return for saving themselves. Starvation made people desperate.

"I might even get ye an ale instead of the piss water the guards are providing ye with."

He was silent for several moments, and I could see in his eyes he was genuinely considering my offer. But then his face hardened and he glared straight into my eyes. Damn. Allan o' the Wisp was strong-willed. Willing to die for his cause. A shame..

"Ye canna bribe me. I'd rather cut out my own tongue then tell ye what ye want to know."

I leapt forward, reached through the bars and pulled him close to me, my dirk pricking the skin beside his lips. A drop of crimson beaded on his dirty, stubbled face. "I can make that happen."

"Do it," Allan said through gritted teeth.

"Nay," I said with a laugh filled with threat instead of humor. "I'll not take away your ability to speak just yet. But I am going to make ye suffer." I trailed the point of my knife up to the corner of his eye. "I promise, ye will not enjoy it."

I shoved Allan away and called to the guard. "Make our guest comfortable."

The guard smiled, no doubt thrilled to mete out his chilling fantasies with Allan, a stark contrast to his usual job of standing watch in the dark of the dungeon.

"Keep him alive," I ordered. "Enjoy your stay, Allan 'o the Wisp. I'll be seeing ye again soon."

Part of me prayed that the threat of a beating would change his mind, but it didn't. He stood still, proud, while the guard unlocked the door.

I'd be lying to myself if I didna admit how angry the devil made me. I'd get no information from him, and I doubted his goons knew anything. MacDonald wouldn't trust this kind of information with a man simply pushed to siege. They weren't the brains behind MacDonald's machinations. Simply pawns.

I needed a swim. Had to work this out in my mind.

I stole unseen through the corridors and down the stairs to the water gate. The men nodded to me, but didna attempt to engage me, knowing by my glower when I tread this route, I had no interest in communicating with them.

Down the narrow path I went until I came to the cut of stone leading down to the beach. The beach was empty. I stripped off everything save the knives strapped at my wrists. Wouldna do to be attacked without weapons to protect myself—not that I couldna take a man's life with my bare hands.

The water felt cool to my skin, lapping away some of the tension. But mostly giving me a chance to think. I had to decipher who was the best to spread the rumor with. Who was most likely an enemy among us. A thought I found most disconcerting. It could be anyone.

Emma mentioned she'd seen men running across the fields toward the trebuchet. 'Haps she would be able to identify them in person. The men were out in force trolling the woods. The slugs weren't intelligent, they'd make a mistake and my men would find them.

But that didn't help me in choosing men now.

I sliced through the water with each stroke, feeling my muscles work, bunching and then lengthening. Across the loch, one of our docked ships rocked at its moor. The others were safely hidden in natural cut alcoves.

Mayhap the best way to draw out the enemy was to offer them something they couldna refuse. The ultimate prize—the kingdom.

Energy burst through my limbs and I pumped toward the shore. Forgoing my *leine* and boots, I tossed on my plaid. Victory in sight, I needed to set things to right with Emma. Ewan would wake soon and then we'd need to question the men. But thoughts of the lass only made my blood burn with lust. She was the only woman who could slake my needs.

A thought I'd ponder more on later.

I tossed my hair, sprinkles of cold water sluicing over my skin and set out at a jog toward the keep.

But what I found—or rather the lack of—sent my blood to chilling.

Emma was nowhere to be seen.

CHAPTER SIX

Emma

Just the wind.

Nothing more.

I tried not to panic, convincing myself a little bit of darkness never hurt anyone. I ignored the chills of warning skating over my skin. Bending to feel the ground beneath my fingertips, I met with dusty, cool stone. I set the candelabra down and plucked the tinderbox from my bodice, its sharp-edged metal a comfort in this place.

How had Logan used it before? Feeling along the edges, I opened the box, revealing the piece of flint and the metal tinder to my touch. He'd just scraped them together. A spark had flown. I could do this. People had been lighting fires for thousands of years. It couldn't be that hard. Easier than rubbing wood together.

I felt for the candles, making sure the wick was near the flint and tinder. I realized with a striking dread, this was going to be harder than I thought. With a fire, there was so much more for the spark of flame to hit against in hopes of catching — here I had but a small inch of thin wick.

"Please, please, please light," I mumbled, striking the flint and tinder. A huge spark lit the dark, but quickly faded giving me a flash of the cobweb covered stone walls. Before I could spot a spider I was in the dark again. I prayed the spider whose cobwebs those belonged to, wasn't too big or too poisonous.

Well, at least I knew how to get the spark. Positive thoughts. This was simply going to take a bit of finesse, but I would get it done. I held the flint closer to where I believed the candle was and struck again. The sound echoed ominously through the stairwell, and once more the darkened cavern illuminated for a second. My mind played tricks on me. Showing me demons in those rapid bursts of light.

"No," I whispered. There were no demons here, just an overactive imagination and a rising fear of darkened spaces.

I struck again. "Please, God, let this work!"

Luck — or God — was on my side. The spark caught the wick, greedily burning, and melting the wax at its nape. My shoulders sagged with relief. I let out the breath I'd held and allowed myself a moment to collect my bearings. I'd not realized how much I'd worked myself up.

I tucked the flint and tinder back into the box, stuffing it back between my breasts. Using the lit candle, I touched the flame to one other, saving the remaining two in case these candles burned completely through. Had to save my resources.

Time to face my fears.

I held the candelabra up, my legs shaking slightly, and stared into the dark. The stairs were only lit about ten paces in front of me, leaving the rest to my scared imagination.

"Just a castle. No such thing as…"

As what? I'd thought there was no such thing as time-travel and look where I was. Not believing in something hadn't helped in the past. And before I would have said there was more of a likelihood of there being ghosts than time-travel. Shit. That meant there were definitely ghosts down here.

As if the ghosts heard me, a soft breeze, like breath blew across my neck. *Shit. Shit. Shit.*

"Please let me pass," I said instead, hoping to strike a bargain with any would-be ghosties and goblins.

Good lord, I was becoming ridiculous. With a nervous laugh, I took a step forward, my foot sliding down one stair, and then the other. With each ensuing step, the stairwell lit all the more, easing the fear and tension knotting in my belly. Until I turned around and saw that the way I'd come was as dark as a moonless sky.

The stairs seemed endless, as though I were descending into the core of the Earth. They just kept going. About ten steps and then a turn, making me dizzy as I went, I felt like I was going in circles.

At last, what seemed like hours later, I hit the last stair and the candles dimly lit a single, small round chamber. The space looked to only span about six feet in circumference. In the center of the small room was a rather tall square, wooden table. Nothing was on it. No chairs either. But what was most interesting was the four, imposing doors, each graced with a large iron lock.

And I had no key.

I set the candelabra on the table, noting that my two candles were nearly burned through, and made my way to the first of the doors. Dust covered the lock, and when I touched it, even in the dim light I could see the streak of black I created on its surface. The air was stale, and I imagined it smelled much the same as a crypt.

I recoiled, hands held to my chest. Maybe this was a crypt and behind the locked doors were hundreds of bodies. Bones upon bones. The air became harder to breathe.

Swallowing hard, I took a step back, doubting my reasoning for venturing down here. What was I thinking? I turned in a circle, taking in the thick, locked doors.

I had no place being here. Logan would shit a brick if he knew I was down here. And all that talk of trust we'd just had. It was now officially out the window... If he caught me down here, there was no way he'd give me his trust. If he didn't catch me, I was bound to drown in guilt for having gone behind his back.

I had no place being in Gealach, or this era for that matter. And yet I was. And so I had to deal with it. I was already down here. There was no going back. I shoved aside my good conscience. No use in dwelling on what would happen when I encountered Logan now. I'd cross that bridge when I came to it.

I had to face my fears in order to learn from them, to grow. So I stepped back to the door. Studied it closely, realizing that beneath a layer of time, there were carvings much like those on the bed posts in mine and Logan's room. I traced my fingers over them. Celtic runes, designs in swirls and knots. Warriors, animals, weapons, battles, feasts. Carvings into the wood like the paintings on ancient Egyptian walls. The engravings looked to tell a story, a history, just like the ones on our beds. Not similar, exactly. At least, I thought. God, it was like a game of clue, and I wanted desperately to get behind those doors to see what the answer was. What did they mean?

Questions I would undoubtedly never know the answers to.

"Ugh," I groaned with frustration, the noise oddly mute in the tiny circular room.

I yanked on the lock, just to check. No luck. The darn thing was securely locked. Even still, I checked each one. All locked. I shoved against each door with my shoulder, thinking perhaps with age, the wood might easily give way. None did. And all I gained from it was a bruised shoulder. I slid my fingers along the edges of each door frame and along the legs and underside of the table, hoping to find a key. Zilch.

With no key, there was nothing I could do down here. No answers or clues I could reveal. Hands on my hips, I huffed a breath and turned in a slow circle, wondering if I'd missed a hiding place where I might find a key or a clue. Anything. But I came up empty handed.

I had to go back up. Had to figure out where the keys to these doors were.

The light dimmed, and I turned toward the candelabra to see one of the candles had snuffed itself out and the second was close to doing so as well. The wax was melted nearly through, the limp wick sagging to the side. I lifted one of the unlit candles and held it to the flames just in time, as it transferred its life to the unlit candle.

If I didn't hurry to the top, I wouldn't make it before the last two burned through. I was ready to get out of there anyway. To breathe in fresh air. The creep factor of this place was eating away at my nerves. Lifting the candelabra, I took a hurried step forward. My toes grazed the stairs, misjudging enough to pitch me forward.

Instinct bade me to put my hands out in front of me, and at the last second I realized I'd let go of the candelabra in the process. It clattered somewhere to my left, the candles instantly snuffed.

"Dammit," I muttered. My hands stung from where I'd landed, the jarring sting racing up my forearms.

Pitch black. As if it hadn't been bad enough down here already. I patted my chest. Still had the flint. Just needed to find one candle. Only one. And then get the hell out of here.

I crawled to the left, hands splayed out, feeling along the dirt-packed floor for the candles. They couldn't have rolled so far away, and yet it seemed they did. Or that the floor had opened up and swallowed them whole. Anger sliced through me, sweat beaded on my upper lip. *Clumsy fool.* I could hear Steven's voice in my head, telling me what an idiot I was. How could one person manage to screw up so royally? Down here in a dungeon in the dark.

My hands slid over tiny pebbles, dirt, and other things I wasn't sure I wanted to know about—spiders, rats, bones. But no candles.

"God dammit!" I shouted. It made me feel a little better, but in all reality, part of me waited for some evil spirit to answer me.

I had to keep trying. A second later my head banged against the wall. No candles. No candelabra. I could be crawling around the floor of this cell for the next week with no luck. At least with the wall, I could find my way to the stairs and there was only one way to go—up.

I stood, keeping my hands against the wall and felt my way around. One door. I pushed back my fear, pretended I was playing a game with my eyes closed, not that I was blinded by the pitch black and possibly already in my grave. Moments later my hands hit air and I stumbled forward onto the steps, my knees taking a particular beating.

Thank God for the stairs.

I started to crawl up, but running would get me there faster. It'd seemed to take forever to come down, had to be at least a hundred stairs. Counting would keep my mind off the dark. And so I lifted my skirt in one hand, kept the other on the wall to my left, and climbed.

One. Two. Three. Four. Five... Ninety-seven. Ninety-eight. Ninety-nine.

"One-hundr—"

Once more, I stumbled forward, my foot landing on nothing as I'd lifted it to hit another stair. Falling, I prayed I wouldn't tumble the hundred steps back down. The plummet would surely kill me.

Crack.

The sound reverberated through my ears and my teeth crunched together as my head hit hard against the stones of a landing. Momentarily stunned, I could do nothing but lie on the ground, and stare into the blackness, willing myself not to pass out as pain seared through my head.

With trembling fingertips, I palpated my forehead where I'd hit the wall. Warmth oozed from a gash.

Great. I had no idea where I was, and now I was injured. Bleeding. And…

I couldn't concentrate. Suddenly yawning wide and suddenly so tired. Dizziness made my eyes roll and my mouth was unexpectedly watery. I rolled onto my side, pretty sure I was about to pass out and not wanting to choke on my vomit.

Several more big yawns and I felt myself slipping… sinking into the blackness that surrounded me. Welcoming the dark.

CHAPTER SEVEN

Logan

"Emma!" The rafters of the entry hall could have shaken with the force of my bellow. The muscles of my neck strained, hands clenched and I didna care who heard, or thought it odd that I shouted our guest's name.

Outside dark clouds fused, swirling, the Gods of the skies coming together to rage against those who walked the earth. Lightning cracked and thunder rolled. Yet another storm. Gods with a vengeance against us mere mortals.

With each ensuing tempest, I'd observed Emma growing more distraught. Face paled, eyes crinkled, lips pinched. Nature's rages troubled her. Oft she looked ready to tell me some great secret, 'haps to confess her fears of thunder and lightning. I always sought to take her fear away — kiss her, make love to her. Now, with the skies opening up above us, I wasn't

there to comfort her. I was almost certain she was in a panic —
and now so was I.

Heart pounded, blood roaring loudly in my ears. I had to
find her. Make sure she was all right. The intensity of my need
disturbed me greatly, but I couldna push it away. My skin
crawled, itching to find her. Instinct bade me do it quick. Deep
in my bones I felt she needed me.

A loud boom of thunder rumbled, shaking the earth. This
storm was rougher than most. Another crack and one of the
female servants screamed. The gale was close, as though it
raged above us, and only us. Gealach was a magnet, a target.

"Emma!" I crashed into the great hall again, amazingly
empty. The tables shone, floors were swept and fresh rushes
strewn on the planks. The hearth was disturbingly barren of
flame. Not even a dog lounged, waiting for a scrap.

Gealach appeared deserted.

Where the hell was Emma?

Not in her chamber, not in mine. Not in the great hall, the
kitchens or the garderobe. The gardens were empty of her
willowy physique, and the courtyard and stables held no sign of
her.

I checked them all — twice. Pounding through the keep and
grounds like a man crazed, and garnering the curious glances of
more than one clan member. Those I asked, did not know where
she'd been, or gone to. No one had seen her or talked to her.
'Twas as though she'd disappeared into thin air.

She couldn't have run away. There was nowhere to run,
and I would have been notified if she tried. Yet, I kept recalling
the last words I uttered to her — *You'll be the death of me.*

Mo creach... If she took me seriously then she might have
made an escape somehow. She'd had plenty of time to explore.
I'd taken her down to the water gate before. The lass knew the
way to the ships. But the men would not have allowed
her...unless they succumbed to her charm like I had. The

woman had a way of looking a man in the eye and making him feel that she could see all the way to his soul. Captivated him. Intoxicated him. I couldna be the only one affected by her.

Scrubbing a hand over my face, I cursed the fates.

"My laird." Ewan stepped into the great hall, approaching me with steady steps. The man looked refreshed and he couldna have napped more than a couple hours.

"Not now," I growled, turning away in dismissal.

"'Haps I can help ye find what ye're looking for?"

I glanced over at Ewan. Should I punch him or dismiss him? A good blow might teach the man to never question me. But, hell, I needed Ewan. Hitting him wouldna do me any good. "Nay. Ye're supposed to be resting. Why are ye stalking me instead?"

"I'm nay tired, and a couple of the men told me they had concern for ye."

I grunted, both annoyed and pleased my men felt the need to see to my well-being. "I'm not a bairn, Ewan."

Ewan shook his head slowly, hands crossing behind his back as he stood at attention. "Aye, I know it."

"Then get ye gone."

"Are ye looking for the lass?"

"What?" I settled my hands on my hips. How did he hit it so close to home? Did the man nay understand the words coming from my mouth? "Did I speak in a foreign tongue? I said get ye gone."

A twinkle entered Ewan's eye. I could have belted him. "Och, my laird, I know, but if ye are looking for her, let me help ye so the men dinna think ye've lost your…sense."

I thumped toward Ewan, chest puffed and looked him straight in the eye as I bared my teeth. "My sense?"

Ewan didna back down. He stood taller and spoke in low tones, "Aye, laird. They think ye've gone soft for the lady."

Exactly what I'd had been denying to myself. I backed away a step, my insides exposed. "She's gone." And 'haps that was for the best. I'd never let bedding a woman — or multiple women — get in the way of my ruling the clan, safe-guarding Scotland. One step from Emma and my whole world was beginning to revolve around her. For heaven's sake, if I caught the scent of her as she walked by I scurried after her like a dog chasing a bitch.

"How long?" Ewan's brow wrinkled. The man was oblivious to my ire.

I shook my head, the rush that had been flowing through my blood starting to dissipate. "I dinna know. I saw her last before I went to swim."

"'Tis not possible for her to have left, is it?"

"If she did, someone would have seen."

"Unless she was taken."

"Taken?" The internal response was almost instantaneous. Rage, hot and fierce grabbed me by the ballocks and bade me respond. My hand found its way to the sword hilt at my hip.

"Aye."

"MacDonald." The name came out a curse through my clenched teeth.

"I can think of no other."

A clanswoman came into the great hall from the buttery, setting new candles within the candelabras on the trestle table.

"Have ye seen Lady Emma?" Ewan asked before I had the chance. And good thing, too. Saved me from having to justify to myself why I cared so much.

"Nay, sir." Her gaze fell on me for the first time. She wetted her lips and her gaze roved over me. Plump in all the right places, I'd bedded her before. She wasn't half bad, rather bouncy if, I recall. I still had yet to dress from my swim. Barefoot and bare-chested. Hunger sizzled in her eyes, but I frowned and she turned away toward the hearth, an odd expression on her face.

"What troubles ye?" I asked, trying to sound bored, though sweat trickled over my brow with the force of keeping my calm. And I hoped she didn't answer 'twas only her heightened arousal.

"The candelabra is gone."

"Candelabra?" Ewan asked.

Who the bloody hell cared about a damn candelabra?

"Aye, sir."

Ewan walked toward the servant, but I had no interest in helping her figure out where the missing piece was. For bloody ballock's sake, we had dozens of them. It was her job to keep track, not a warrior's.

While they discussed household supplies I glowered at the tapestry most prized by the Grant clan. The one of the king bestowing a gift on the man I thought was my father. The man I grew up calling Da, and the man who taught me to be a man. The man who turned out to be only a servant of the king, entreated to look over me in the guise of a sire. I still remember that day. My seventeenth birthday, and the king came, his gift to me a golden ring with a giant ruby, which graced my middle finger even now. His gift had also been a curse. Much like the gift received by my Da—the prize of Scotland. His gift was not only me, but a chest buried deep within the bowels of the castle. Fifty feet below ground, in the dark, guarded by demons. Or at least that's what I'd believed as a child. Hell was below the castle, was it not? Fifty feet down got a lad close enough to the fires of Hades to feel the soles of his feet burning.

I could feel it now, singeing my toes.

I needed to have a face to face with James—my king, my brother. It'd been too long. The less I knew what I protected, the more my loyalties were beginning to falter. For certes, I was one-hundred percent loyal to my country, to my people. But I was not and never would be, loyal to MacDonald. The man seemed intent on taking the country for himself. And my brother had yet to ask me to stop him. If anything, James seemed intent on letting MacDonald have his way. The man would have to wrench Scotland from my bloody, dead fingers — and it'd have to be in Hell, because there was no way he was going to outlive me.

A muffled cry sounded in the distance. Pain-filled and desperate.

Emma?

"Did ye hear that?" I asked, turning in a wide circle, taking in the hidden alcoves and noting them empty.

"What?" Ewan inquired.

"I heard a moan."

Ewan chuckled. "Sure it wasn't one of the warriors rutting a maid?"

The female servant gasped, and pretended to be busy with the candles again, though I could sense by the cock of her ear she was more interested in what naughty things could be happening.

"Could have been." The men were a randy sort and the maids all too willing to comply.

The sound came again. Ewan frowned.

"Doesna sound like pleasure," I said. Where was it coming from?

"Sounds like 'tis in the walls."

"Aye." There was silence. No other sound issued. "Demons."

Ewan chuckled again. "Demon nymphs."

I sat down on a bench beside one of the trestle tables where the rest of my garments had been folded neatly by some discreet servant. I slipped on my woolen hose and boots, feet feeling confined. Sturdy. Controlled. I unpinned my plaid, letting it fall, and got another gasp from the lass. I grinned wickedly, turned around and winked. If she was going to see my bare arse, at least she'd have a story to give her friends.

I tossed on my *leine* shirt, and re-pleated my plaid, belting and pinning it into place. Ewan handed me each of my weapons and with each one I put on, the more controlled I felt. More like myself. Claymore strapped to my back, broadsword at my side. *Sgian dubh* in my boot, knives strapped to my wrists and another above my knee. Ready to take on the world if need be — and it would be soon.

"I need to send out missives to our allies and one to the king." I walked toward the arched door that led up a set of stairs to my library.

"And so it begins," Ewan said.

"Aye. As we discussed." Emma was nowhere to be seen. I was beginning to think she'd wanted to disappear. Searching for her was only going to drive me crazy.

Ewan nodded and headed in the other direction. He'd start the rumors about men departing on ships and others heading into the woods on foot. Soon we'd know who could be trusted and who couldna.

When my foot hit the stair, the muffled cry sounded again. I turned around, having thought the noise came from the middle of the great hall. Something was wrong, for I knew we were nay haunted by ghosts.

"Logan..." I swear to sky, my name was uttered.

"Emma?" I called. Was it she? I couldna tell by the voice, but my gut drew the inevitable conclusion. It had to be her. "Emma!"

"Help..." The word was quiet, hushed and hidden.

"Where are ye?" I called.

The maid stood, hands over her mouth staring toward the tapestry. Ewan came back into the great hall, eyes narrowed.

"Here..."

Her voice was weak, pain-filled.

"My laird, there." The maid pointed toward the tapestry.

With long, rushed strides I made it across the great hall and whipped the tapestry aside, hearing the sounds of metal and stone crunching, and then, *pling pling pling,* as the tapestry came unhooked from the bolts and fell in an echoing whoosh to the floor.

The door.

The one door I'd avoided as a child, and still as an adult. The one that led to Hell beneath Gealach.

"Emma," I whispered, stepping up to the stone wall, and sliding my fingers over the stones, remembering exactly which one to push to make the door open.

The stone sank into itself and with a flip of the hook, the door opened silently, the light of the great hall making a slow beam in the darkness, and lighting on a figure lying on the ground.

"*Mo creach!*" I crouched down and scooped her up, blood covering her hair, forehead and trickling down the side of her face. She was covered in dirt and looked badly beaten. "Who did this?"

Her limp hand fluttered up to touch my face, and her eyes blinked weakly open. "You found me."

"Aye, lass. What happened?" *Mo creach...* I'd given up on her. Was about to begin the war without having looked further. She was hurt and I was trying to forget about her. I felt like an utter demon myself. Her injuries were no one's fault but my own. I should have protected her.

"Logan," she mumbled, eyes closing tight as she lost consciousness.

My eyes flashed up at Ewan. "Get Cook. Looks like her head needs to be stitched." To the maid, I ordered, "A bath. She needs to be bathed."

Both of them rushed to do my bidding and I took the stairs two at a time to Emma's chamber. Who had hit her? Stuffed her in the hidden staircase to never be seen again?

Had the workings of MacDonald all over it. Someone didna want Emma found. The same person who tore her nightrail to shreds.

"I'll never let anyone hurt ye, again," I swore.

She slept peacefully against my shoulder. Her face pale, and dark circles beneath her eyes. Her chamber was empty, didna looked to be disturbed. I settled her on the bed, on top of the coverlets, and made a quick round of the room to be sure no lurkers hid in wait for their chance to strike. All clear, I dipped a linen square that sat on her side table into the basin of waiting water and wiped at the blood on her cheek, temple and around the laceration just above her hairline.

Dear God, who had done this?

The wound looked deep, but not jagged. Would be easily stitched.

Emma groaned, her head lolling to the side. Her arms flailed and I gripped her hands in one of mine as I finished cleaning away the blood.

"Shh, love. I'll nay let anyone hurt ye."

"Logan," she murmured, her eyes still closed. "I knew you would save me."

"Aye, love. I'll always save ye."

I let go of her hands for a moment to rinse out the linen before touching it to her wound again. It seeped a small amount of blood, but looked to be thinning.

Tiny hands gripped my wrist, and she did open her eyes. They were wide, red, and caught my gaze.

"I'm sorry," she said.

"Sorry? Dinna be sorry. I'll make whoever took ye pay with their life. Who hurt ye?"

"Don't kill me," she whispered.

"Lass, I'd nay harm a hair on your head. Who did this?"

She shook her head. "I did it."

I kissed her fingertips. "Ye dinna need to protect anyone."

"No. I'm not protecting anyone. I fell. It was so dark."

I bent lower and kissed her lips, dry and cracked. "Rest my darling. Ye're confused."

Her eyes widened and she pushed against me. "Logan," her voice was steady, stronger. She tried to push up on her elbows, but I nudged her back down, taking hold of her hands. "I'm not confused. I went through the secret door. My candles blew out and I fell in the dark. Hit my head on a wall."

Her confession took a lot from her and she sank fully against the pillows, a rush of air coming from her lips. But it also took a lot from me. My chest seized.

"Ye willfully went into the wall?" I narrowed my brows, disbelieving what I was hearing.

"Yes."

"Why?"

"I wanted to explore. To find answers."

I dropped her hands and pushed back from the bed. "Answers to what questions?" My voice came out harsher than I wanted.

Emma reached for me, and I felt compelled to step closer, but forced myself to remain rooted in place.

"I was curious. I found the door when I first came, but was too scared to go down the stairs. I..." She bit her lip, closed her eyes for a brief moment before fully opening them again. "I want to know your secrets, Logan. You keep so much of yourself hidden from me. You make me feel like... I don't know. I thought..." She sighed. "It was stupid. I know."

"Stupid doesna begin to describe your actions. How many times have ye cheated death today?"

She cracked a small smile. "At least twice."

The curve of her lips enchanted me each time. I wanted to pull her into my arms, devour her.

"I have secrets because without them, death would envelop us all. Dinna go into the wall again." It was as much and as little as I'd ever tell her.

By now, I knew I could trust that Emma wasn't sent here to kill me, to steal the treasure. But what I couldna trust was that Fate had not sent her here to steal my heart and soul. Both of which were no longer mine. Instead, they hung on a thin line of twine between the two of us and each day came closer and closer to being fully hers.

I loved her. Had confessed it once as we made love, but never allowed myself to put forth such revealing words again. Emma was my future. My all.

"Dinna go behind the wall again. Ever," I repeated.

She nodded. "I am bound to you," she whispered.

Her words ripped at my chest, sinking myself that much deeper into her.

CHAPTER EIGHT

Emma

In the distance, a piper blew his melodic tones over the fields and moors. The enchanting music echoed off the stone walls of Gealach Castle. Magical in quality, the wailing cries of the bagpipes could have been from some unearthly creature, drawing everyone within hearing distance into its haunting web and thieving their souls.

I was drawn to it, lulled into a meditative state. Coupled with the warmth of the bath, the soft strokes of the soapy cloth over my back, Logan's deep and throaty murmurings, I was halfway to heaven.

"Sit back," he whispered.

I leaned against the back of the tub, steam rising up around me. Kneeling behind the tub, Logan slid his hands over my shoulders, sloping downward toward my breasts, nipples just visible above the water. My body hummed for him. Completely relaxed, his touch was just as melodious as the pipes, luring me in, singing to my soul. Enough to make the ache in my head dim. I arched my back, my breasts rising above the water and into his waiting hands. He stroked them gently, rubbing his thumbs over my nipples. My skin puckered, even with the warmth of the water. No amount of outer heat could stop the chill of need his touch created. An oxymoron really. He made me hot and tingly, and yet I shivered and had goosebumps.

"You're not supposed to service me," I said, sliding my hands over his forearms. As laird of his castle, it was custom for Logan to be served by others, but he frequently turned the tables.

Logan chuckled. "Och, lass, dinna be fooled. 'Tis as much a service to me as it is to ye."

I smiled. My eyes closed as I laid my head back against his muscled chest. It was such a comfort to be with him, in his arms, his presence. An escape from every reality—past, present, future. When we were together, everything disappeared. There was no distant, vengeful husband searching the world for me, preparing a brutal punishment. There was no medieval war. No one trying to harm me. No demons beneath the castle. Just two people, madly into each other, and boundless pleasure.

And completely unrealistic. We couldn't just stay here in this room together forever, as much as I wanted to. There was a world outside of this room. A life outside of pleasure, and I had no idea where I fit, and whether I did at all. I'd been trying. The clan seemed more apt to take me in, allowing me to help in the gardens, and occasionally with mending a shirt or some other chore. Logan, too. When I was with him, I felt like I belonged. But all the same, pounding in the back of my head was a warning.

This wasn't my time, my place. Logan was a laird, important in his realm. There were things like arranged marriages, and all, to contend with. Weren't there?

Ugh. Marriage.

Logan may have once told me he loved me. Told me today that he'd always protect me. But that didn't mean that he was going to marry me. And was he even allowed? Weren't there rules? Was it a sin if we did marry, since I was essentially already married, even if my husband didn't *yet* exist? If I married Logan now, there would be no future self to meet Steven. *That* marriage didn't exist. So, that meant I was free, didn't it?

Oh, my God. Why did I care? Why was I ruining this awesome moment with thoughts of marriage, worries of Logan's future wife?

Because reality was something that always tried to make a dent in the fantasy I was living in. At any moment, I could wake up next to Steven, my nightmare complete. My stomach caved in on itself. This would all come to an end, and I'd be heartbroken.

I bit my lip, tried to force myself not to feel Logan's fingers trailing over my belly and dipping between my legs. Tried my best not to lift my hips in invitation, because doing so was continuing with this fantasy when I really should be forcing myself into reality.

Failed.

A stifled moan escaped me. Painful almost in its need to be quiet. The muscles of my sex clenched around his invading fingers. I wanted this, but I shouldn't. Oh, God, how I craved it.

"Why so tense, love?" he whispered against my ear. "Relax."

His words were a potent drug, lulling me once more into that meditative state where thoughts were artless and sensation was penetrating.

I wanted to obey him.

I spread my legs, knees parting, and warm water lapping against my swollen folds.

"That's right, open for me."

Anything he wanted…

My knees fell against the sides of the tub, and I relented, letting him have his way. Thick fingers delved inside my most sensitive parts, playing, toying, eliciting such frantic jolts of pleasure, I held my breath to keep from coming. But holding one's breath rarely ceased an orgasm from ripping one apart. When Logan flicked his index finger over my swollen clit, he prompted a rampant domino effect I had no control over — possibly because I'd worked so hard against it.

Orgasm took hold of me and whipped me around in overwhelming pleasure-filled hands. I clenched tight to Logan's hands which held my breasts, letting his gift take hold of me. Unable to stop what was happening. I desperately prayed for it to never end. My hips bucked upward, knees jammed so tight against the sides of the tub I was bound to be bruised. I rode his hand, rode the climax, crying out with little care as to who heard.

Logan seized my mouth in a jarring kiss — his tongue delving deep, teeth scraping over my lips — swallowing my cries of pleasure.

"Och, lass, ye're so passionate." Logan stood behind me, walked around to the side of the tub and held out his hands, pulling me to stand.

I shivered as the cool air of the chamber hit my heated skin. He didn't move to cover me, or hand me the towel folded neatly beside the tub. Instead, he took a step back and just looked at me. I resisted the urge to rub my hands over my arms, to smooth my puckered flesh. I let him look, watched his eyes dilate as desire filled him. Felt my bodies reaction all the more. My breaths were shallow, quick. Heart racing.

"Gealach has done well by ye." His gaze roved over me in appreciation, rolling from my face, my breasts, belly, sex, thighs, on down to my toes. Logan reached out and traced his fingers, feather-light, over the sides of my breasts, the curve of my hip, around to my buttocks. "Turn around."

I did as he asked, feeling completely exposed, but wanting nothing more than to please him. Afraid of slipping in the watery tub, I turned slowly, the warm water lapping at my calves.

I sensed him step closer to me. The heat of his body teased my back.

"Aye, done well." He cupped my buttocks in both hands. Coarse, warm, palms and fingers, massaged the muscles, the flesh that I knew was fuller than four months ago. "Your arse is perfect for grabbing hold," Logan said gruffly.

I'd come to Gealach thin as a rail—a result of Steven limiting my diet, and a belly too worry sick to eat. I looked down, seeing, really *seeing*, for the first time that my breasts were fuller. Hips swelled and my legs no longer resembling sticks. A few months of hearty food and lots of good sex had indeed done my body well. I wasn't so pale I could see my veins, though I'd not spent an overlarge amount of time in the sun. It was simply that I was healthier. My skin had a glow to it.

I blew out a breath. "I'm happy that I please you."

"Oh, Emma, ye more than please me."

He pulled my damp hair to the side, exposing my shoulder and neck to his mouth, and grazed his teeth over my flesh, licking away the droplets of water. "Ye taste so good."

I wanted to sink back against him, but feared I'd lose my balance. My knees were locked, and all I could do was sigh as he explored my buttocks. His fingers delved into the crack, sliding gently up and then back down. Each time he scraped the pad of his finger over the sensitive pucker, I jerked, gasped. No one had ever touched me there, not even Steven. A shimmer of fear gleamed on the recesses of my mind, but because this was my Logan, and I trusted him, I forced it to remain there instead of surging forward.

"Do ye like that?" he asked, pushing gently on the star of my ass.

I nodded, biting my lip.

"I want to hear ye say it."

He loved to hear me tell him how much I wanted him, liked his touch. I didn't know whether it was because he was genuinely concerned about whether or not he was doing the right thing, or because he liked being in control and hearing the shake in my voice because pleasure had hijacked my vocal cords.

"I like it."

He slid a finger inside my slick sex, and then back up my ass to the center where he pushed, gently. A spark of pleasure and pain ignited at the source, tingling outward. He pressed a little harder, so that his finger was maybe an inch inside me.

"So tight," he whispered, nipping at my shoulder. "I want to fuck ye here." Logan pulled out his finger and replaced it with something larger, more velvet. His cock.

My breath caught. I wanted his cock buried in my forbidden place and abhorred it at the same time.

"Do you want me to?" he asked.

He was putting this in my hands. Asking me what I wanted. Giving me the power to say no. That made me want it all the more. My clit tingled, and I squeezed my thighs, knees quaking at the thought and sudden onslaught of desire.

I nodded. "Do you have…"

"Oil?" he asked.

I nodded. Oil, lube, same difference. No KY here.

Logan lifted me from the tub and dried me from head to toe, only to wet me again with his tongue from my neck to my ankles where I stood. He slid his wicked mouth over me, kissing, licking, nipping until I quivered and crooned. Then he laid me on the bed.

"I'll get the oil."

I nodded, legs shaking. I bit my lip and watched him disappear through the door that connected our rooms only to return a moment later with a small wooden bottle with a cork in it. He lifted the little bottle and winked. Crawling onto the bed, he knelt beside me.

"Are ye certain?" His brows wrinkled together in concern.

I smiled, worried that my face showed how nervous I was. I had gotten used to hiding my emotions with Steven, but with Logan I couldn't hide anything. I was an open book to him. Exposed and easily read.

And the truth was, I *was* nervous. Scared, even—not that he would do something to hurt me, but...

Anal sex was so much more than regular sex. A violation of a part of me I'd never thought as sexual. Never wanted anyone to look at, let alone find pleasure in. Yet, with Logan, as with all things, this was different. If I was going to experience anal, I wanted it to be with him. I trusted him. Knew he would stop if I asked.

"If ye want me to stop, I will." He caressed my thighs, tickling me with his tender touch, almost like he read my mind.

"I know."

"Ye do?"

"I trust you."

Logan gave a satisfied smile. "Good."

Now it was my turn to show him. I rolled over onto my belly, leaned up on my elbows and looked behind me. "Show me what it's like."

I could see Logan's throat move as he swallowed. Watched his pupils dilate and eyes darken. He loved to dominate me, but loved it even more when I asked for it.

"With pleasure," he said, voice gravelly.

He stroked his hands over my buttocks, massaging, gripping, opening them and exposing my heated star to the cool air. I let out a little whimper, and he'd yet to do a thing. But it was as much mental as it was physical. Every part of me tingled. My sex throbbed, dripped. My clit felt like it was on fire. My nerves were on edge. Even his breath on my skin set me closer to climaxing. I squeezed my eyes shut and laid back down, leaning my forehead onto my folded hands.

"Are ye all right?"

"Yes," I murmured.

I heard the sound of the cork being wrenched free—a little pop—and then warm, slick hands rubbed over my buttocks and lower back, then the backs of my thighs. I let myself sink into the pleasure of his massage, moaning at nearly every roll of his hands.

Then I heard a sound I loved—the click of his buckle and the thump of his clothes falling to the floor. I imagined him behind me, tan skin covering his brawny physique, a sprinkle of dark, crisp hair on his chest arrowing down to a jutting, thick cock. He would be kneeling, the muscles in his thighs and abs flexed. Jaw clenched, eyes riveted on my ass—which I lifted into the air in offer.

He gripped my hips and pulled me backward, his cockhead nudging between my oiled cheeks. I shivered, and pushed back, decidedly ready to take on this new lesson in pleasure.

"Not yet, lass."

Gently, Logan pressed me onto the bed, his hands pressed to either side of me, he loomed over me, just barely touching his front to my back. He kissed me gently on the shoulders, swiping away my hair to kiss my neck and nibble my ear.

"It pleases me to have your trust." He kissed the side of my mouth and I turned so I he could have full access to my lips, which he took advantage of.

"You've proven yourself trustworthy," I said a little breathlessly.

He sank his hips against my buttocks, sliding his body up and down the length of me, the oil making it a new, slick and hot sensation.

My fingers curled into the coverlet, a bit of sheet bunched between each as I tried to restrain myself from crying out, from levitating off the bed. It was glorious, heat and ecstasy. And so simple — just the sliding of his hard, sinewy body against mine. He wasn't even inside me. I'd never thought something so simple could be so good. There had to be something in the oil. It was hot, warm, and so freaking amazing. I teetered on the edge of exploding.

"With ye, each time feels like new." Logan spoke against my ear sending a fresh shiver racing through me.

I hated to ask how many others he'd done this with.

"Ye react with such raw, primal passion," he crooned, nipping at my earlobe.

I shivered and pushed my hips up and back, searching out his cock. I didn't care where he put it, as long as he put it in and pushed me over the edge.

He pulled back, lifting off of me, and I felt the loss of his warmth keenly.

"Come back," I murmured.

Logan chuckled. "I ought to leave ye wanting."

"No, why?" I bit the coverlet as his hands, slickened with oil, slid over my buttocks and down the crack.

He was preparing me. He wouldn't leave me wanting.

"Only because ye beg for it. I should like to think about ye dripping wet, your cunt clenching for what I didna give ye. Hell, the thought has me harder than stone."

He pushed his cock against my wet folds, and then thrust forward. I cried out, rocking back against him.

"Don't leave me," I moaned, rolling my hips, begging for him to move, but he stayed still, buried deep inside me.

"When ye move like that, it feels so damn good. Do it again."

I obeyed his commands, rolling my hips, and squeezing my eyes shut. I felt my sex slide along his cock and then back, moving myself up and down his length.

Logan's fingers dug into my hips, stilling me.

"Now 'tis time." He slipped his cock from my sex and guided it along my virgin crevice. "Relax."

I took a deep, shuddering breath, trying to relax, though I was strung taut as a bow. I unfurled my fingers from the sheets, reaching behind me to grab onto his thighs.

"Are ye ready?" he asked.

"Yes."

Logan centered his cock on my tight ring, pushing lightly. I could feel my body resisting, squeezing tight and not allowing him to enter.

He stroked his hands over my back, massaging the muscles of my spine. "Relax, love. Let your muscles go loose."

Somehow, I was able to do it. I sank against the bed, and as I did so, he glided in an inch or so.

"That's it, lass." He groaned, his hands tightening around my waist, then my hips, and my ass.

He sank further in, and instead of the pain I thought I'd feel, there was an intense pleasure. Logan stayed unmoving, his breathing ragged.

"Are ye well, love?"

"Oh, yes." My eyes opened and stared into the candle lit room. "Better than well."

He moved slowly, his pace steady, not frantic. With each fixed stroke, the frissons sparking from somewhere deep inside and outward grew. My breathing turned just as ragged as

Logan's and I was once again clutching at the sheets, but somehow remaining relaxed elsewhere, allowing him entry.

I knew he kept his movements calm and gentle for me. Afraid he might hurt me. But… I was suddenly filled with the need for ferocity, for him to take my ass and pound me. I wiggled beneath him, trying to encourage him to move faster, deeper.

"Och, dinna move like that," he said.

"I want…" I trailed off, unsure of how to ask him. To beg him.

"What do ye want?" Logan's voice was ragged and his thighs trembled next to mine.

"I want… more."

"Dinna say that." His fingers gripped so tight to my hips, I reveled in the pleasure pain.

"I do. I want you to…" Oh, my God, I was going to say it. "I want you to fuck me harder. Faster."

"Nay, lass, I canna." But he did. He pushed a little deeper, two strokes faster. "I dinna want to hurt ye."

I moaned as he gave me a taste of what I wanted. "It doesn't hurt. It feels… so good."

"Aye. Bloody hell!" He reached around the front of me, teasing open my folds, his fingers circling my clit with furious strokes as he drove deeper inside me, his pace quickening.

"Yes!" I cried out. This was what I wanted. I gasped, loud, nearly choking on it. Consumed with pleasure. I pushed back against him, wanting to take him in deeper, to feel him filling me up completely.

Logan had conquered me in so many ways, and now here was yet another way he completely laid me bare. Flayed me open.

The pleasure was so incredibly intense, tears welled in my eyes. I blinked them back, gasping and moaning, and tearing at the sheets.

"Come, Emma."

"Yes! Yes!" I cried, desperately striving to do his bidding.

"Now, Emma!"

There was no holding back. No amount of gasping or grinding my teeth. My body was not my own. It belonged to Logan and it did exactly as he commanded, when he commanded it.

White shot before my eyes as pleasure fired a violent rocket through me. I was going to pass out. I couldn't breathe the pleasure was so powerful, concentrated. And yet, it was everywhere, in my fingers and toes, the backs of my knees and especially between my thighs and the crack of my ass.

My elbows buckled, and I started to fall forward, but Logan held me up, pushing further inside, faster, harder. Abruptly, he withdrew, rubbing his cock against my buttocks. I felt his hand moving at lightning speed as he stroked himself, and then liquid heat shot against my ass. Hot, sticky, sweet.

I tumbled to the sweaty sheets with an audible exhale, and Logan collapsed half on top of me, half beside me.

"Wow," I murmured, unable to form anything more coherent.

Logan pulled me into his arms and kissed my lips. "Ye're amazing, Emma."

He stared into my eyes for a long time. Long enough that I thought he'd confess his love for me. I hadn't realized until then how much I longed to hear it. To tell him, too, how much he meant to me. That I never wanted to leave and would he have me for more than a lover.

But he didn't say anything. And neither did I.

CHAPTER NINE

Emma

A younger warrior, arms full of freshly crafted arrows, hurried past me in the courtyard, dropping several along the way, into the mire that stewed where grass no longer grew, and the scattered hay had missed. His hair flew in wild, unkempt clumps, and I had a feeling, judging by the untidy pleats in his tartan, that he'd had one heck of a rough day already.

"Hey, wait!" I called, bending to pick up the abandoned arrows, slickened with mud from yet another storm.

The young man didn't turn around. Didn't pause in his steps. There was no more commotion in the courtyard than any other day. Wood being chopped, metal clinking, dogs barking, children running, men and women talking and carts moving—but my voice wasn't so low that it was drowned out by all that.

Frowning, I followed the warrior. Where could he be headed in such a rush that he didn't care for his cargo?

Darn, but he was fast. Walking hurriedly in skirts didn't exactly go so well for me. The fabric twisted and turned, getting caught up between my ankles and knees. My shoes threatened the hem with each step. My clothes were going to trap me, trip me up. How did anyone in a medieval gown get anything done quickly? I lifted my skirt out of the way with one hand, the other still clutching at the arrows and ran after the man.

What was his name? I studied the back of his head—curly red hair. Had to be late teens. Ugh. I'd seen him around, but couldn't pull his name from wherever it lay buried.

"Hey!" I called, hoping to gain his attention. I waved the arrows at the back of his rushed body, hoping anyone standing between us would help, but they didn't.

Every bystander simply looked at me like I'd lost my head. And I couldn't really blame them. After all, I was running through the mud, splatters flicking up into my face, waving arrows like a madwoman. As if the inhabitants of Gealach didn't already think me crazy…

The last seventy-two hours had been filled with moments like this. Everyone at Gealach was rushing this way and that. Repairing and preparing.

The gaping hole in the castle wall from MacDonald's trebuchet was already repaired, the stones whiter, cleaner in that spot than anywhere else. No lichen or moss growing on the mortar and stones.

What they were preparing for, I'd not the privilege to be informed. Logan was knee deep in missives, messengers, meetings with his men, all within his library—which I saw yesterday on the one occasion I dared to visit after asking Ewan to take me there specifically. I wasn't willing to risk near death again.

When I'd popped my head in, he'd looked up at me, bags under his eyes, making it obvious that he'd not been sleeping. Ink stained his fingers, and papers were raveled and unraveled all around him on the surface of the desk where we'd made love. A messenger stood in wait in the corner and another approached while I was there. Hard to think of it as our little love haven when what it exuded now was an important man dealing with important matters.

Logan told me he was simply arranging for the inevitable. He'd then told me he would speak with me about it later. I'd assumed that meant he would be visiting me in my chamber, but he never arrived, and when I'd tried to sneak between our two rooms I found his chamber empty, cold and his bed made. It was the same in the morning. He'd not slept there. A very brief moment of jealousy passed when I wondered whose bed he had slept in, but I knew that was ridiculous. The man wasn't sleeping. Probably was up all night in his library.

Three days since we'd really talked. Three days since he'd made love to me. Three days and I was starting to feel insanity creep its way in. A problem I would have to remedy. There were going to be many days like this one. In an era fraught with unrest, what more could I expect? This was Logan's world, his legacy. He was going to protect it with savagery until the day he passed on. I would, too, if I were in his shoes.

"I can take those, my lady."

Ewan stepped into my line of vision, halting me in mid-step. I struggled a fraction of a second with my balance, and my gown. Then handed him the fistful of arrows.

"Ewan, I didn't see you there." I wiped the dirt off on the apron I wore over my gown as I'd been on my way to the gardens to help with picking herbs for drying.

He gave a slight shake of his head and smiled. "Ye looked intent on catching the lad."

"Well, he dropped these, and when I called out to him, he didn't bother to stop."

Ewan chuckled. "Youth. They are so easily distracted."

I smiled, watching Ewan wipe the mud from his fingers onto this plaid.

"Thank ye for picking these up. Could have been dangerous." His gaze flicked behind me, and then roved to the sides as if the images of what danger could have occurred flashed in his mind's eye.

"You're welcome," my voice trailed off. I had the distinct feeling that wherever the *lad* was taking the arrows, Ewan—or more correctly, Logan—didn't want me to see. Maybe Ewan wasn't imagining disaster so much as he was trying to see who else was watching.

"I'll make sure these are joined with their mates." His smile was contagious, and I knew he was trying to divert me.

In my old life, I, Mrs. Gordon, would have nodded and scurried away. But that wasn't me anymore. I was someone new, here. A woman who did ask questions and didn't take no for an answer.

"What's going on, Ewan? I've barely seen Logan at all in three days, and the people are running around as though preparing for an apocalypse. Please, tell me."

Ewan's expression looked bored. The men of Gealach were so infuriating in their ability to hide their emotions and thoughts. "Tell ye what?"

I held out my arms in exasperation. "Everything."

"Well, as it turns out, we are preparing the clan. Fortifying the castle. 'Tis a task that takes much concentration and many hours of work. That could be the reason ye've not seen much of the laird lately. I'm afraid I haven't seen much of him, either."

"Preparing the clan for what?"

Trouble was brewing. I could feel it in my veins, circling in the air around me. Ewan met my gaze briefly before turning to nod at another young warrior who ran by with an armload of pikes.

"War." The way he said it… so matter of fact, as though he were mentioning dinner or a walk in the gardens. Normal. Without question.

Maybe for him it was standard, but not for me. The mention of war meant thousands of people dying, children going hungry, plagues breaking out from the filth of so many people bunched together, dead bodies leaking their decaying poisons into the water… Nausea made my belly roll.

I had a freaking boatload of questions. "War?" I could barely get the word out. "Here?"

He shrugged. Crossed his arms over his chest. I could see I wasn't going to get many answers out of Ewan, and really, I couldn't blame him. It wasn't his place. He would consider it a front to his laird to give me information without checking first.

I groaned my frustration and put my hands on my hips — then promptly realized what I was doing. Holy crap, I'd completely changed. Gone was the shy slip of a woman who first fell down the stairs of Gealach, replaced by a woman, strong enough to give what for to a fully armed warrior — and one I wasn't involved with. Almost like I was mistress of this place. Ludicrous.

Letting my hands fall limp to my sides, I lifted my chin — stubborn apparently a new trait of mine, as well — and stared Ewan straight in the eyes, shocked once more with familiarity. He was so much like my brother. Yet, I knew it wasn't Trey. Trey was gone and there was no coming back from the dead. Unless…

"Where do you hail from?" I asked, wanting to get more to the bottom of my thoughts on his origins. Had he fallen from the future, too?

"The Highlands, my lady," he asked with a quizzical raise of his brow.

I resisted the urge to roll my eyes. "I know that, Ewan. What part?"

"Ah, Gealach. I grew up here."

"So you've known the laird your whole life?"

He frowned at me. "It would seem so."

A vague answer. Was it possible he didn't know? "And your parents?"

He stiffened. "Gone to their reward. If ye'll excuse me." Ewan turned on his heel and marched in the direction the younger warriors had taken, without waiting for my reply.

Obviously, his parents were a touchy subject, and I wondered if that had anything to do with the fact, he might not actually remember them, or what happened. I just couldn't shake the feeling that Ewan was, in fact, Trey or part of him, at the least. If I could travel through time, then couldn't my brother? If Trey did... where were my parents?

Oh, it was all so silly. Time-travel simply couldn't be another of Gealach's secrets. This castle's secrets were all buried in a dungeon, not a time warp. I must have just been a blip in the grand scheme of things.

A thought struck me—what if Logan was avoiding me because of what happened with me and the secret panel? He'd not talked to me about it since it happened.

I had to find him. Had to clear things up between us. I couldn't bear the thought of him going to war and nothing being resolved before he left.

I headed back to the castle, hoping to find Logan on my way. I didn't want to venture to his office, afraid I might get stabbed for real this time. If it were modern times, the man would have a hell of a lot of workman's comp issues to deal with.

"Logan?" I called, upon entering the grand foyer.

Silence and blank stares from a few female servants sweeping the floors, were my only response.

"Have you seen, his lairdship?" I asked, realizing I'd just called their master out by his first name—a major faux pas on my part.

Two shook their heads and another stepped forward, eyes cannily looking into mine and pointing toward the stairs. "He's just gone that way."

I didn't know whether to thank her or ask her why she decided to come forward. They'd all obviously seen the way he'd gone.

"Thank you." I decided on kindness. I could always ask questions later.

I lifted the hem of my gown and walked up the circular stairs, stopping at the first floor in hopes of finding Logan there. The corridor was dark and all the doors shut tight.

My footsteps echoed on the freshly swept floors, and shadows bounced over the walls. Only two torches were lit—one near the stairs and another at the far end of the hall. My heart pounded inside my ears, and my breath echoed within my head.

Walking all alone in the darkened hall set me on edge. There were people here out to get me. Prisoners in a dungeon that could be set loose at any moment. No wonder Logan preferred me to stay in my room. Whatever confidence I'd gained outside while talking with Ewan, evaporated.

A dozen steps down the hall, and suddenly I felt like I was being followed. The hair on the back of my neck stood on end, and a shiver stole over me. I stopped walking, listened, hoping to hear something, anything, to put my mind at ease. But silence greeted me. I took a few more steps forward. Someone was definitely walking behind me. Though I couldn't hear their steps, I thought I heard their breath, and I could *feel* them.

Fuck...

I whirled around. Nothing.

God dammit! I hated feeling so scared. So vulnerable.

"Who's there?" I asked, scanning the hall, the darkened nooks between the doors and shuttered windows.

Silence was my only answer.

Well, it was obvious Logan wasn't here. There was no point in continuing my search down this hall. I didn't even know where it led. Best if I just went back up to my room. I could wait until I heard some noise next door. Or ask Agatha to fetch him to me, or something. I wasn't up for exploring. My head was starting to ache, too. I reached up to touch the spot, fingertips meeting the crude stitches that had put me back together.

My stomach knotted, making a gurgling noise and I didn't know if it was because I was nauseous or hungry. It had to be nearing lunch, and I'd not eaten a thing Agatha brought me, preferring instead to read a book Logan gave me, and then to take a leisure walk as far outside as I was allowed to venture — which ended up being not outside of the castle walls — before I was due in the gardens.

With my mind caught up in itself, I didn't hear, but rather felt the approach of someone behind me. Felt the soft breeze of movement on my arm, and then they grabbed me. A strong arm around my middle and a hand over my mouth, stifling my scream.

I kicked, writhed, frantic to get out of his grasp, but he only lifted me into the air and backed further down the hall with me. I was helpless, couldn't get a good enough bite on the hand covering my mouth, but that didn't stop me from continuously trying.

My arms were pinned to my sides, and no matter what I did I couldn't wrench them from my assailant's iron grasp. I arched my back, bucked my hips. Nothing was working. I was stuck. Taken.

Logan had been right.

I was easily overtaken. I felt a little like the boy who cried wolf. I'd not been abducted before, and he thought I was. Now that I was truly disappearing would he come look for me?

Yes. He had to. He would. I had to go on believing that, but even still, I wasn't giving up without a fight.

Going limp, I pretended to pass out. Just as I hoped, my attacker's grip loosened. I gave it another couple of seconds, then went nuts, bucking, twisting, kicking, shouting behind the hand that stifled me.

I had to get free!

The deep rumble of laughter that sounded from the man holding me, made my blood run cold.

"Logan?" I said, though it didn't come out that way. More like, "Mwa-mwa," with his hand covering my mouth.

He set me down and bounced back a couple of steps, his hands held up in surrender when I whirled around. "Well, lass, ye put up one hell of a fight."

"What are you doing?" I asked, incredulous.

"I wanted to see if ye knew how to protect yourself."

"You scared the shit out of me."

He frowned and looked skeptically at my skirt. "Really?"

I groaned, and pressed a hand to my belly, still all twisted up from the scare of being abducted. "It's a figure of speech."

"Odd."

I glared up at him. "What was the point of that?"

"I told ye, I wanted to see if ye could protect yourself."

"And?"

"Ye did a fair enough job, but I still would have gotten away with ye. Tied ye up."

"Then I'm doomed," I said, my tone dull and full of sarcasm.

"Ye might be. Let me tie ye up and teach ye how to get out of the binds."

"I don't know…" My fingers trembled as the adrenaline that had been pumping through me tried to work its way out of my blood.

"Come on. 'Twill be fun. A lass can always benefit from learning how to take care of herself."

"Fine."

Logan's eyes lit up like he'd just been given leave to get off all day long, every day, for the foreseeable future. Hell, hadn't I given him that already? I smirked.

"No funny business."

He looked at me like I had two heads. "There is nothing funny about being bound."

"I hope to never find out."

At that he grinned. His lip curling in that sexy way I liked and he winked, slow and seductive. My body quivered, nipples hardened. Why did he have to do that? Oh, but how I liked it.

"I hope ye do find out… Can be a most pleasurable experience."

"Minus the abduction."

He chuckled. "Aye, there is that."

"Lead me away, sexy kidnapper."

Logan hoisted me over his shoulder and slapped me on the bottom. "I plan to."

CHAPTER TEN

Logan

Emma's arse was soft and pliable beneath my hands. I'd not touched her in days. Forced myself to stay away from her. There were fortifications to take care of. Allies to deliberate with. A war to prepare for. Rumors to spread and weapons to forge. A country to save and a king to keep in power.

I avoided her at all costs mainly because every time she was near, I had to touch her. An incurable disease—this need to feel her beneath my fingertips. But the other reason was my avoidance of what lay between us. Her venture into the secret stair—to the bowels of the castle that housed my treasure, Gealach's treasure. How had she discovered the door?

At first I'd believed that our hidden enemies took her. Beat her. But she'd insisted, and Emma wasn't a good liar. I could read her like an open letter, dissect her as I could a downed kill.

She couldna hide from me, not in anything, and especially not in this. Emma had gone down below of her own accord. And because she was a nosy wench. That much was clear.

No matter, I was going to take this next lesson to prove to her that the best place for her was in her bedchamber. 'Twas safest. Anyone could take her at any moment, especially if she took to slinking around the castle. She was lucky that it was only herself that got her harmed this last time. There was no telling what MacDonald or one of his men would do to her. They were all crude, malicious and ill-tempered. Thought nothing of harming a lass, despoiling them of what they valued most.

"Put me down," Emma said, her breathing labored as I jogged up the stairs to the upper chambers.

"Not a chance, lass."

She slapped my back and wiggled.

"Aye, keep it up. 'Tis exactly as a lass would react when grabbed by a strange man."

She giggled a little and slapped at him again. "But you are no stranger to me, Logan. I know you all too well."

I laughed. "Not well enough." I jogged a little faster. "Ye see, I will only run faster, but never let ye go."

"I was always taught to fight harder. That the more I fought, the more reasons for an attacker leave me be."

"Ye have a point. And I agree. Keep fighting. Never stop. Kick, hit, bite, scream, buck. All of it. If ye can, find out your enemy's agenda. The need for ye. Once ye know the need, ye'll have found his weak spot and ye can manipulate him."

I rounded the last stair and opened the thick door leading to the hall with our chambers.

"And what is your need?" she asked, no longer thumping on my back.

"Ah, now that is for ye to find out." I shoved open the door to my chamber — not hers. "Keep your wits about ye."

With a chuckle, I kicked the door closed and in two strides was across the room. I tossed her onto the bed, watched her bounce and grapple for purchase with the thick coverlet. Her face was flushed, chest heaving, and a smile filled with happiness curled her lips. Hell. The woman was beautiful, intoxicating, and her mood contagious.

Before she had a chance, I leapt onto her with a deep laugh, holding her to the bed — positioning her arms above her head, my thighs on either side of hers pinning them closed.

"Ye're stuck." I grinned, bringing my face within an inch of hers. My nostrils flared as her scent filled me — lemons, flowers, herbs.

Her lips were plush, red, and irresistible. I wanted to kiss her. Taste her to see if she was as sweet a treat as she smelled. Hell, I wanted to pound her through the mattress, but then I'd never get this lesson done. One she needed, given the coming war and the very real possibility she would be taken away from me.

Knowing this helped me to push away, to keep from kissing her, taking her roughly while the bed scraped wildly over the floorboards, until her toes curled and she cried out for more. *Mo creach.* My ballocks swelled with my cock. Both wanting what I was refusing to give myself. Her sweet, slick prize.

Keeping her pinned, I reached beneath the bed for the leather box that held exactly what I needed. Only twelve by four inches, it was easy to grasp. I set it on the bed beside Emma's head and gazed at her to gauge her reaction. She rolled her head to the side, staring at the box.

"What's inside?" Her eyes were wide with a mixture of curiosity and fear. Beneath me, she trembled, and her palms were a little damp within my grasp.

"Close your eyes."

"No." She shook her head and wriggled beneath me. Her hair had come loose and tendrils stuck to her temples. "I wouldn't close my eyes against an assailant."

"Och, ye're right. Keep them open." I unclipped the latch and lifted the lid, revealing the black velvet interior, filled with silken ropes—a gift from my brother on one of his many giving days.

Bribes, really, meant to keep me in my place. And when once sexual implements and beautiful women were enough, I knew now my brother, my king, would need to offer me much more to keep me pleased.

Emma stared at the box, but from her vantage point she wouldna be able to see inside. She bit her lip. I know she wanted to ask, but she didna.

"Ask me." I grinned with challenge, my cock rock hard.

Her gaze slid back to mine, eyes tempting me. "Would an attacker wait for me to ask?"

"Ah, ye're correct once more."

I pulled my sgian dubh from my boot and touched the tip to her bodice.

"What...?" She didn't seem able to get the rest of her words out.

"Just what any rogue attacker would." I slit her bodice down to her waist, revealing creamy, soft flesh. It was enough to make any man give up every possession he owned just to touch her.

"Logan! I needed this gown."

"I'll get ye another." I tugged the cut clothing away, yanking at her gown, hose and boots, until she was completely nude upon my bed.

With her fully naked, I climbed back on top of her, my thighs straddling her. God, how I wanted to yank off my own garments and ravish her, but that wasn't the point of this exercise. But first I had to wipe that frown away. I bent to kiss her, but she turned her head away.

"I wouldn't kiss my attacker willingly."

"What about unwillingly?" I nibbled along her chin.

"If he was as handsome as you, I might be persuaded."

I ignored the roll of jealousy in my gut, and instead captured her mouth with a possessive kiss. "Is that enough persuasion?"

"Oh, yes."

I grinned. "Good. But your attacker most likely willna be as handsome as I, nor as good a kisser."

"And I won't want to kiss him naked either." She smiled prettily up at me. "These lips are reserved for only you."

Mo creach... The lesson. The lesson. The lesson. I had to repeat it, else forget about it and make love to her right here and now.

I unpinned her legs enough to roll her over onto her belly, before clamping down again. Sweet heaven... Her arse was perfectly round, pink and begged to be kissed. I pulled her hands behind her back, forcing myself, unsuccessfully, to stop staring at her sculpted rear. Emma whimpered.

Leaning down, I whispered against the shell of her ear. "Are ye afraid."

"Never with you."

"Maybe ye should be."

And I meant it in more ways than simply the physical sense. We were both in so deep... emotionally. Words I never thought to think. Emotions of that kind had no place in my world — anger, pride, a sense of brotherhood, those were things I was allowed to feel. But... the deep, intense feelings I had for Emma were taking over my entire world.

"Maybe you're right," she answered back.

Time to stop this line of talk, else her lesson would be postponed while I made love to her instead of uttering the words.

I pulled out a thin, black, silken cord and slid it over her arms to her wrists.

"Your attacker will tie ye at the wrists." I started to wrap the cords around her dainty wrists, being cautious not to tie too tight. "Only they willna be as gentle as I am."

"Don't be gentle." Her words were shocking, but so was her tone — breathy, sensual.

Emma liked what I was doing to her. Good God, what a woman I'd found. When I'd bound her wrists with the belt for the first time some months before, she'd enjoyed it, as she had several other times since. But this... I'd not expected...

Hell... When I'd said she was going to be the death of me, I wasn't lying. The woman was going to kill off every bit of sense I had.

I tightened the bindings. Not enough to cut off blood flow, but just enough to pinch. Then I backed my way down her legs to her ankles, rubbing the curved muscles of her calves. Emma had soft skin. Flesh that beckoned. I couldna help myself in taking a taste, bending over to nibble at the indentation behind her knee. She moaned, her fingers clasping at the ties.

I pressed her ankles together, smoothing a thumb down the center of each foot, over the arcs. Her toes curled with the movement. With a sigh, I wrapped another set of silken cords around them, fastening her legs together. I flicked my gaze to her face and caught my breath. She licked her lips, eyes wide and watching. Her breath quickened.

She wiggled her arse, and all I could think about was how she let me slip inside that tiny, tight, hole. How she'd begged me to give it to her roughly. This little, timid lass who'd come to me months before, weakened and abused. Having been here for so little time, it was amazing the transformation she'd made. Emma was strong, aggressive even. The intelligent, clever woman who'd been hidden had been allowed to bloom here.

"All tied up now," I murmured. "How does it feel?"

"I know it was supposed to be a lesson in escape," she answered, her voice throaty, taking on an edge of desire. "But with you..."

I grinned. I knew what she meant. It was sexual, heated. My cock was hard, aching with the need to push inside her tight, wet cunt.

"With me, what?" I asked, sliding my hand up her thigh, stopping when the tips of my fingers touched on the wetness of her sex. She was drenched.

"With you, I find I like it," she admitted, squeezing her eyes shut slightly, then reopening them.

That admission took a lot from her. Almost like she hated to acknowledge something like that about herself.

"There is nothing wrong with that." I toyed with her hard little nub of her pleasure, watched her eyes roll a little as she gasped.

"Really?"

"Nay, lass. What do yet think I have these ties for?"

"I... I don't know." Emma opened her eyes and looked back at me. She pushed her hips back, forcing my fingers deeper inside her.

If I didn't stop now, she'd never learn to escape the ties. "I'll give ye ten minutes to escape. If ye dinna, then I'm going to punish ye."

"Punish me?"

"Aye, love. As I've done before. Leave ye wanting, wet and shivering. Thinking of me the whole rest of the day, your cunt quivering with the need for me to fill it."

"Oh," she murmured, excitement bubbling behind that soft sigh.

Good God, I had to have just one taste. "If ye escape, I'll give ye what ye want." I gripped her hips and lifted her up, exposing her sex to my view. Slick, pink and beautiful. I dipped low, stroking my tongue over the wet folds, the button nub.

Emma moaned, pushed back against me fast. I drove my tongue inside her, reveling in the power of giving her pleasure, and knowing there was nothing she could do about it. And then mourning the fact that I was also losing control.

One last lick, and then I backed off the bed. Putting distance between us, leaving her wanting, though my cock hated me for it. The front of my plaid was tented, the soft wool scratching frustratingly against my cockhead.

"Ten minutes," I repeated.

"Okay," she said, breathless.

Emma rubbed her wrists and ankles together, just as anyone would when trying to get loose. The only problem was, the way I tied them, those movements would only tighten the cords over time rather than loosen them.

"That willna work," I said after two minutes. "Ye are running out of time."

Her eyes flashed angrily over at me. What had been sensual was turning frustrating for her. I couldna help but smile. "Try something else," I said.

"Like what?"

"Use your imagination."

"A hint, please?"

"Move around."

"I thought I was."

"Nay, ye were only wiggling. Your captor willna leave ye in a place ye can easily get hold of anything. Use your body to your advantage and figure a way out."

Emma pressed her lips together, determination firing in her eyes.

"Fine."

I smiled. She was accepting the challenge. She scooted her round arse backward, lifted up her chest, so that she knelt on the bed, then walked with her knees over to the side of the mattress.

"How am I doing now?" she asked.

"Better. And I'm enjoying the view."

She stuck her tongue out at me and pushed her arse back at me, accentuating the lovely sight.

Emma glanced down at the floor, and I could almost see her mind scheming. She lay back down on her belly, and wiggled her legs off the side, using her chin to push herself up once her feet touched the floor. She stood, a triumphant smile on her face.

"I did it," she said.

"Not quite there, yet. And ye've got four minutes left."

She narrowed her brows and those plump lips went white as she pressed them hard together. Turning in a circle, she glanced around the room, her eyes lighting on several items before she frowned at each one and continued her search.

When she glanced at the hearth, her face lit up and she began her long, foot scoot over to the hearth. It was hard not to rush toward her when she wobbled, even when she fell hard to the floor. But she rolled to the side at the last minute so her head didna hit. I let out the breath I held and watched her get onto her knees and scoot over that way—much more balanced. When she reached the hearth she turned around, lifting her arms behind her until she found the poker, then maneuvered it so that the poker slid just a half inch between her wrists and the cord.

A pity to see such beautiful, soft cords shredded, but worth it, and I did have several more inside the leather box.

Back and forth she went until the cords split and she cried out with joy when they released. She held her hands up to me, showed me she was free.

"Times up," I said, grinning at her with triumph. "And ye've not yet freed yourself all the way."

"A few more seconds and I would have. That means I still win."

"Nay, lass, not if I were a captor. He'd have lopped ye on the head and tossed ye back abed."

"And what would he had done to me on that bed?" she asked coyly.

I knew what she wanted, what she was asking, but her question put the real thought in my head. MacDonald would torture her. Let his men torture her.

"Nothing ye'd enjoy, I assure ye."

Her smile faltered. "I was only —"

"I know it, love." I stalked forward and untied the knot at her ankle. "Now ye will be punished."

I lifted her from the floor, held her around the waist and pulled her flush against me. Every inch of me screamed to go against my plans. To indeed toss her onto the bed, the floor or up against the wall, and thrust home. But I couldna. That would be to go back on my word. 'Haps...

I pushed her down to her knees and unbuckled my plaid, letting the fabric fall. My cock was hard, raging. "Do ye know what I want?"

She nodded, glanced up at me, her eyes sparkling. Emma licked her lips. "Yes."

"Take hold of me," I said.

She wrapped her long, slim fingers around my shaft. Looking down at her, my cock inches from her face, her hand holding me, it was nearly enough to make me burst, but I held myself in check.

"Open your mouth for me, Emma."

Her silken lips opened, revealing the velvet of her tongue.

"Take me in," I demanded.

Emma closed her eyes and leaned forward, her lips brushing the tip. I hissed a breath. "Open your eyes," I said through teeth gritted in pleasure. "Look at me."

She opened her eyes, her gaze connecting with mine at the same time that she nearly swallowed me whole. Her lips stretched as my cock disappeared into her mouth.

I could barely breathe. Heat, soft and wet enveloped me. She sucked, and sparks of pleasure shot from the tip to the root and then along every nerve in my body. Emma's mouth was a pleasure zone. I was coming undone. Control slipping away with each movement of her mouth and hand. And she knew it. Her eyes locked on mine and she watched me unravel. Sucked me harder, her tongue swirling over the head, rubbing up and down.

Threading my fingers through her hair, I tugged her closer. Jerked my hips, thrusting forward. God, her tongue was magic. She moaned against my cock. I groaned. Forced myself to keep eye contact with her as I fucked her sweet mouth.

"I'm going to come," I growled.

Emma moaned in response and sucked harder, her hand jerking up and down in time with her mouth. I felt it from the base of my spine, a climax so huge, it might have killed me if it weren't for the fact I wanted more. I fisted my hand in her hair, and she cried out a little, but she didna stop, she only went faster, sucked harder, flicked her tongue over the ridge where my shaft met the head of my cock.

"Emma!" I bellowed, bursting inside her mouth.

She moaned, swallowing every last drop, sucking me dry. It only made me harder. I could have kept going. Wanted to lift her up and wrap her legs around my hips, fuck her up against the wall. But I didn't, I let her go, pulled away, my breath ragged.

"Let me feel ye." I demanded.

Emma stood.

"Spread your legs."

She opened for me, standing naked, chest heaving, lips swollen from sucking me, legs spread.

I slid my fingers over her nub, between her slick folds and she shuddered, moaned. Cream coated her, dripping down her thighs.

"I will come for ye, tonight," I said gruffly. "Dinna pleasure yourself. I want ye to stay just as wet as ye are right now."

Emma nodded.

"I'm going to make ye come until ye faint," I promised.

"I can't wait," she said, her lip trembling.

"Och, lass…" I couldna make her wait. I'd done it before. Tortured her with pleasure. But I wanted to see her scream. Now.

I drove my fingers inside her, watched her eyes roll. "I'll give ye release, but I willna take ye. Not like ye want me to."

She closed her eyes, bit her lip and leaned against me, rubbing her hip against my hard cock. I gripped my free hand around the back of her neck and crashed my mouth on hers. Our tongues met in frenzied passion.

Seconds later, her sex gripped me tight, quivering, and she cried out against my lips.

"I dinna know if I'll ever get enough of ye." I slid my lips from her mouth to her neck, kissing her pulse there.

"I'm almost certain I never will."

CHAPTER ELEVEN

Emma

An elephant of enormous proportions filled my bedroom. In fact, there was more than one. They crowded the air, and took the comfort I found in Logan's embrace and crumpled it like trash on the floor beneath their massive feet.

If we didn't talk about the elephants soon, I was sure my brain would eat away at itself with worry and confusion. Both topics that needed to be discussed were hard to broach—the secret chamber I'd found and our evolving relationship.

I loved the games we were playing, the lessons he was teaching me. Enjoyed how we were exploring sensuality in exhilarating different ways. How being here in this time, this castle, and especially with Logan, had changed me. I liked the way I was. The way I was growing, the person I was becoming. I enjoyed it. Truly.

So, why then, did I have to fuck it up?

Talking would ruin the peaceful moment we were sharing, limbs entwined, soft caresses and sweet quiet.

Why did I have to get all emotional and put a name to what we had and go directly against Logan's wishes? There wasn't supposed to be more to us than this. Yeah, sure, no contract was signed, but it was spelled out carefully. Lovers. Nothing more, and no less.

But it felt different—this thing between us. I knew it was different. Just like I was.

I guess defining what we were to each other just went with the territory. I was changing, and in changing I had to be sure of what and who I was, and where I was, and my place here. Especially with Logan. I was completely and utterly in love with him. Wholly obsessed with him. A sweet obsession. One I never wanted to be rid of, and yet I knew it couldn't last if I let these elephants keep stomping around. My confidence in myself as a woman was nearly whole. I'd bared myself to Logan— mostly. And I was ready to take that plunge, to flay myself wide open, if he was willing to do it with me.

Logan lay beside me, his breathing calmed in the aftermath of our encounter. His chest rose and fell, and I swirled my fingers in the crisp hair covering his muscled pecs. "Logan?" My voice came out sounding timid, exactly the opposite of how I wanted. I flicked my gaze up to study his chiseled profile.

"Aye?" His tone was guarded, and he stiffened slightly beside me, but his expression didn't change.

I bit my lip contemplating how to reply. The man knew me well, and he could most likely gauge what I was going to ask, or maybe at least had an idea.

"What was down there?"

His hand around my back tightened, and the muscle in his jaw clenched for half a second. "Down where?"

113

Already I wanted to pull the words back. This conversation was doomed to be unpleasant. Logan was withdrawn naturally and even with the closeness we'd developed I'd not been able to crack his mortar shell. I closed my eyes, and prayed he didn't strike out at me—not physically, I could never be afraid of him in that way, but mentally. I didn't want him to push me away, and yet I needed answers.

"The stairs…behind the wall."

"Ye should not have gone down there." Even tone, no inflection, just a simple phrase laced with warning.

He didn't move. His breathing slowed, despite the slight quickening of his heartbeat beneath my fingertips.

"I…" I swallowed against the dryness of my throat. "I know."

"Then why did ye?" He was pulling the conversation away from where I'd led it. And yet, he was pointing in a direction I'd wondered why he'd steered away from before.

"I needed to know. I was compelled." Yes. That was the truth. I was compelled to go down and explore. Just like I was now in asking him to explain.

"Compelled?"

I chanced a glance up at him. The muscles of his jaw worked, tightening, then loosening again and again. His lips were thinned a little and his eyes were steadily regarding me.

"How does one become compelled to enter places they should not?"

His question seemed to have an obvious answer. Doesn't someone always want to go where they are told not to? And perhaps if they don't physically want to go there, they are curious about it in any case?

"Logan, there are so many secrets here." I leaned up on my elbow so I could look him more closely in the eye. His gaze was guarded, but still I forged ahead. "You don't tell me anything. I

114

feel like I'm in a maze, doomed to forever hit dead ends without discovering the way out."

Eyes darkened, Logan studied me for a long time without speaking.

"Have you been in many mazes?"

I couldn't help laughing, his question seemed so absurd. "No."

Logan turned his eyes up to the ceiling, his fingers making whorls on my back. Did his body language mean he was not as disturbed as he appeared?

"Gealach is a great mystery to many. And it remains that way for its own safety, and the safety of its people."

"I am not a threat. I promise you." I couldn't help the desperate edge to my words. We took two steps forward, one step back, and I seldom felt like I was getting anywhere. Constantly running in circles. Endlessly stuck in a labyrinth.

He turned back, his face softer. The hard edges still there, but not as tight. Opening up to me again.

"I know it, lass. I know it." He spoke barely above a whisper.

"Then tell me. Please. Don't push me away."

"Dinna go into anymore secret doors, Emma. Ye're lucky to have come out alive."

That I knew. For crying out loud, I thought I was falling down a hundred stairs a few days ago. Someone in the castle wanted my clothes shredded literally—and it wasn't Logan. Then Logan nearly stabbed me with his own sword. There were plenty of dangers. I was lucky to come out of *any* room alive.

"The door ye found, is nay the only secret passage within the castle—and others lead to places far more hazardous. I wouldna want ye to encounter one of the meaner sorts of Gealach. Or a prisoner."

Meaner sorts?

And could he possibly be hinting that a prisoner could escape?

Logan was frowning again. His brows knitted, lips turned down. But even looking so seriously like that, his gaze directed toward the posts of the bed, I found him dangerously handsome. I had to straighten my spine to keep from arching into him for a kiss. Not an easy feat given that I was lying on my side, propped up on one elbow, a leg thrown over his and my hand flat on his chest. His warmth seeped into my fingertips, and the scent of our lovemaking was an aphrodisiac I was more than willing to drink in.

This was no time for kissing. No time for a lesson or a game. The shutters of Logan's mind were being opened, just a crack now, and if I could get my fingers inside and pry them apart just a little more...

"This is a very serious situation, lass. I dinna think ye understand." He swiped a hand over his face, pinched his lips.

Voice strained, a shiver stole down my spine. "What?"

"If ye were a man..." He paused, locked eyes with me. "Ye recall the warrior striped of his clothes and tied to the post?"

"Yes."

"If ye were a man, I'd have Ewan take the angry cat to ye for what ye did." He shook his head. "I wanted to believe that ye were stolen, that ye didna do something so stupid all on your own."

My mouth fell open, the pit of my stomach burning like I'd swallowed a lump of coal. I'd never felt Logan's anger like this. Feared its direction landing on me, but never truly had it. It was frightening, but not in a scared rabbit running sort of way, but in a devastating way. I hated to disappoint him. Hated for him to be angry at me. Hated that he would even say those words.

Logan pulled away from me, sat forward on the bed and swung his legs over to the side. An icy grip found its way around my throat. That hot piece of coal in my belly quickly turned to ice. I could hear the man's screams in my mind, the sharp crack of the whip, and I jerked forward as though the nine horrid tails had slapped wickedly over my skin. I must have moaned. I heard the sound of it and Logan must have, too. He flicked his gaze around.

"I'll not do it, Emma. Even if I should."

I'd known that. Well, had hoped it. But it was still a huge relief to hear him say the words. To know that he didn't truly wish me harm. But that didn't make his displeasure in me go away.

"More than just ye and I know about where ye were. There was a maid there. Then there was the Cook who stitched ye up. They will expect me to react."

What little relief I'd felt blew off with the wind. What was he saying? That he wouldn't go through with it, but he'd make sure someone else did, to teach me a lesson or to set an example?

My throat went tight, and I reached up to touch my neck. My fingers trembled against the base of my throat. The man I loved and trusted, stood, his nude body rigid with anger.

"Why did ye have to do it? Why could ye not leave well enough alone? Did ye nay realize what danger it would be to go into a darkened stairwell guarded by a secret entrance? What the hell were ye thinking?" He rounded on me, naked, glorious and massively angry.

I could do nothing but stare up into his rage-filled eyes.

"I thought the MacDonald took ye. That one of the prisoners escaped and took ye. That the one who cut your nightrail found ye and had ye stashed away where he did God knows what to ye. I was scared, Emma. Ye scared the bloody piss out of me."

I inhaled sharply, held my breath in my lungs until it stung. He was scared. I scared him. This great powerful man, full of control, never letting his emotions get in the way of him… He was frightened.

I climbed from the bed and hurried with shaky legs the few feet to him, wrapped my arms around him and sank into his unbending form.

"I'm so sorry," I whispered. I pulled back enough to search his face. "I never meant to scare you. I know it was stupid. I know I shouldn't have done it. But I wanted answers. Hoped that maybe, whatever I found down there would give me some clue as to who you are. I know you, Logan. I know your soul, but I don't know much *about* you."

Logan's nostrils flared as he sharply inhaled.

"What?" I dared ask, worried, I'd said the wrong thing.

"Ye are…" He gritted his teeth, baring them as he tried to keep in whatever was about to spill from his lips.

"Tell me."

He gripped my face with both of his hands, holding me in his stare. His fingers were warm, and his thumbs tenderly stroked my cheeks. I gripped his calloused hands, holding him, waiting.

"Ye are the first person who ever…cared." He said it with such genuine sincerity it made my heart melt.

I had to tell him. Had to reinforce that I not only cared for him, but that I loved him. "I love you. Being here with you has been one of the most eye-opening, exhilarating times in my life. You showed me who I want to be. Who I can be. What I want out of life—and most of all, you showed me love. I fell in love with you, hard."

His fingers tightened around mine, his eyes locked fiercely and intently onto my gaze. My heart kicked up its pace and if I moved I swore it would leap right into my throat.

Logan worked his lips but words didn't come out, and then finally, "I told ye before—" He swallowed. "Months ago—" He couldn't seem to finish his sentences, and I knew why, felt that same heated knot in my chest that was so hard to let out.

"I know," I said, giving him a way out. A reprieve from having to bare himself to me. For some odd reason, I felt freer, lighter, more whole, when I told him exactly how I felt.

Logan nodded, his lips pressed in a firm line. "Ye know."

I nodded, sensing his need to keep the words hidden, though emotion shined in his eyes.

"And I'm sorry." I shook my head. "I won't go into any more hidden doors."

"Good. Verra good."

A forceful, single knock jarred us both.

"I am summoned." Logan frowned all the more. "For a moment everything but you and I disappeared."

"Yes." I flashed him a smile. He understood me, how I felt, and he felt the same way.

"Name yourself," Logan called through the door as he dressed.

There was no answer, which only made him hurry his movements, and in turn caused me to hurry in tossing my own clothes on. He kissed me briefly.

"We must part, but I'll be eager for tonight when I can see ye again."

My heart melted. He was opening up to me.

"I'll think of hardly anything else."

He flashed me a sexy, wicked grin, then reached for the door. When Logan opened the door, a small knife was stuck dead center on the outside of it. Both of our smiles faltered, and a cold, dreadful shiver stole over me.

Someone knew we'd been in there together. God knows how long they'd listened. But they'd been angry enough to leave a sign—a note of their disapproval and what they wanted. They wanted me dead. Or him. Or us both, I didn't know.

My blood ran cold, and the murderous look on Logan's handsome face was enough to freeze me in place and wish for mercy on the one who did the deed.

CHAPTER TWELVE

Emma

"**B**ar the door." Logan didn't wait for my response, but disappeared down the hallway.

Too frightened to ignore his warning, I hastily shut the door and lifted the large wooden slab into the two iron holders, barring the door from anyone who would enter. Satisfied no one would be able to bump it out of place, I rushed to the door that separated our two rooms, opened it and barred Logan's door, too.

Safely behind locked doors, for now, I sat on the edge of my bed and stared wide-eyed at the heavy planking keeping an enemy from entering. But it was only made from wood. If someone really wanted to get in they could. All they had to do was hack away at it with an axe.

"Wow." I was struck speechless.

This was no game. This would only end in violence. A whiplash of reality hit, nearly tossing me to the floor. These were treacherous times, and this castle brimmed with danger. I was a coward, wishing for just a moment that I could go back to my own time and be done fearing for my life. Was there any way I could drag Logan back with me?

Did the good outweigh the bad?

I didn't know. I shook my head, so uncertain. And it didn't really matter what my opinion was anyway, because Fate had not deemed it right for me to return home, yet. I was changed. A new woman. What other lesson could be learned — other than the sexual kind Logan was such an expert teacher in — that would keep me here? If I was going off the epitaph that all things happened for a reason, what *was* that reason?

I busied myself in making up the bed, tidying our love nest. Hiding the fact that two people had been in this bed. Fluffing the pillows last, I sat back down, stared down at my trembling hands.

Then an idea struck me. Maybe it was my knowledge of the future that brought me here. Was I supposed to teach Logan something and not the other way around? Did I hold an answer to the secrets of this place and not even know it? I couldn't even imagine what it would be.

I scooted down onto the floor, my butt hitting the woolen carpet, my back plastered to the footboard, and I hugged my knees to my chest. What part of history would I know? I barely remembered high school, and when I'd visited Gealach with Steven I'd been too preoccupied with his sense of disapproval than taking notes about my surroundings. But there had to be something. Even a small inkling of knowledge that could help Logan.

Closing my eyes, I tried to force myself back to that day. Starting with what I wore. Beige...dull... I felt lifeless, looked the part. Steven was particularly unhappy with my hair that day. Had threatened to cut it all off if I didn't figure out how to style it in a way that wouldn't embarrass him. His mother had been with us. They walked arm in arm in front of me, while I hung back—actually relieved the majority of the time. When I didn't feel relief at them being five or so feet in front of me, paying me no attention, I was filled with anxiety for fear of what Steven would say for having not paid enough attention to him.

I evened my breathing, the way I'd learned to do the couple of yoga classes I'd taken. Tried to find that meditative state that would help transport me. I was almost there.

Deep…even…breaths.

The tour guide's voice buzzed in my mind. I couldn't hear what she said, but knew she was there. We were passing through a darkened hallway and she was pointing inside a few rooms that had opened doors and roping to keep us from entering. One looked very much like an office. Old, dusty, leather-bound books filled ornately carved wooden cases. A long trestle table set out like a scene from history. Maps rolled out, mugs of frothy-looking ale, and a papier-mâché mannequin stood in his plaid looking down over a rolled parchment. History stilled.

The guide pointed to a hole in the wall, said it must have been for keeping an eye out on those who walked by.

No. The woman was wrong. That was Logan's office, and I now knew that slot was for a sword, not an eyeball.

We kept on walking and she stopped at a spot in the hallway. Was talking with great enthusiasm, and most seemed fairly interested in what she had to say, but not Steven and his mother—and since I was too obsessed with what they thought, neither did I.

It seemed like now this was a most important piece of information. Like if I knew what the tour guide was saying I'd be able to answer so many questions. I zeroed in on the tour guide. I had to have picked up on at least a few of the words she said. God, what did she say?

Something about a grand escape. Laird Grant. The anger of the king. A great war.

Dear God, I had to tell Logan. Had to warn him somehow.

His prisoners were going to escape.

Logan

"**I** want every person within the walls of Gealach in the great hall. Now."

Ewan gave a curt nod and went to do as I instructed. He was just as aghast with my revelation about the knife in Emma's door.

I paced the length of the hearth, a small, banked fire letting off a small amount of heat. Enough to battle the drafts Gealach was famous for. Come winter, we'd all have icicles on our noses.

I stopped mid-stride and scrubbed a hand over my face. I was deeply troubled.

My love for Emma was going to get us both killed. A love I couldn't even get past my lips. She was distracting me from my *once* only reasons to live—to protect Scotland and the secret of Gealach. The lass was a new addition to that list.

She'd given me another reason to live and one that interfered with the first two. For how could I live to love and cherish her when my life was constantly on the line?

I drew in a deep breath, my gaze driven to the tapestry which hid the secret panel. The tapestry of the previous king and my guardian mocked me. I turned away from the woven history and faced the hearth, empty and barren as my soul.

Servants and clansmen slowly filled the great hall. They stood shoulder to shoulder, boot to boot, eyes haunted and silence on their lips. Their faces were solemn. When I studied them, some looked at me expectantly, locking eyes, and others looked toward the ground. It was hard to decipher who was loyal and who was not, as their devotion could go either way. Looking toward the ground could be a sign of respect, just as it was a sign of traitorous virtues. Openly studying me was likewise hard to decipher. Could be fear of discovery, open hostility. Could also be curiosity as to why I pulled them away from their daily routine.

A quarter hour later, Ewan entered the back of the great hall and nodded in my direction. This was as many as would be present. Looked to be most of them. Those in the field or scouting would be hard to rally just now.

"Clansmen and women, I've gathered ye here for two verra important matters." The buzzing of those who'd chatted while waiting for me to speak silenced. "I'm certain ye've noticed the preparations the men have been undergoing. While we at Gealach are made of hearty stuff and used to the constant tests our enemies put to us, we will soon be greeted with the ultimate challenge. I know ye'll all be ready when it arrives."

The majority of those in attendance nodded, even with panic crossing their features.

I crossed my arms over my chest and regarded the crowd of people. Hoped they could mirror my confidence. "Now to the other matter. There have been a series of threats against myself and other members of this household." No need for me to give Emma's name away. Besides, there were bound to be those who still did not accept her as part of us, even if she'd been there for months and had my full protection. "I dinna take these threats kindly. Nor will they be ignored. If ye know who has done it, or ye've been the culprit, come and speak to me at once. The punishment will be lessened if ye confess. Confess not, and expect to feel the full extent of my ire on your traitorous back."

A sudden rush of movement caught my attention. I searched the crowd to find Emma pushing her way through. Her eyes were wide, as though she'd seen a ghost, and a frantic air surrounded her.

"My laird!" she called. "I must speak with you."

What the devil? Had I not just finished thinking about how the woman was distracting me from my task? Here she was in the flesh interrupting my business with the clan, and yet I felt my love for her tighten my chest, the sudden need to grab onto her and find out what had her so riled. But that wouldn't do.

"Emma, go back to your chamber," I ordered, giving her a stern look. I couldn't have anyone in this room thinking she could interrupt me so easily. Think me to have gone soft.

Emma faltered in her steps, her face stricken as she looked up at me. "But—"

"Go back to your chamber." I fairly snarled the words at her.

And though it pained me to see her turn away, shoulders slumped, dejection shining in her eyes, I had no other choice. Whispers were already heard bouncing around the room, high-pitched drivel I couldna decipher, but could likely guess at their content.

Once she'd disappeared again, I cleared my throat loud enough that the hushed tones died down and once more I had the attention of the clan.

"Go back to your duties, and if ye've anything to tell, come to me or Ewan."

The people bowed their heads and began to file out of the great hall. Their grumbling murmur's filling the rafters. Not one stayed behind.

For cock's sake, I needed an ale. As if hearing my thoughts Ewan pushed a mug into my hands.

"Well handled, my laird."

I grunted and took a long gulp. One mug wasn't going to fix this.

"What do ye think the lady wanted?" Ewan nodded to a few men who walked by.

"I dinna know."

"Curious that she'd come storming into the room. Seemed urgent." The man sipped casually at his ale.

It did. And I was…uncomfortable with it. I didn't want to admit, even to myself, that I was fearful of her urgency. I'd already admitted once today that I was scared of something. And warriors weren't supposed to be fearful of anything. We accepted our fates and dealt with what the Lord deemed fit to provide us.

"My laird?" Ewan shifted uncomfortably.

I downed the remaining ale in my mug. "What is it?"

"Would ye rather I go and see what has your guest…excited?"

Damn. I blew out a breath. Part of me wanted to go to her, but I knew at this moment, I had the clan and battle to muddle through. 'Twould be best if Ewan went to see what Emma needed. The distraction wouldna bode well. Ewan and Emma seemed to have formed a bond—nothing like the one she and I had formed. More like the bond of blood ties. I was grateful she'd been able to make a connection with a few people. Made her feel more useful, and made me feel better about her days not being spent alone and cooped up in her chamber.

"Aye. If ye would. I'll go and tend to the waiting messengers."

Ewan nodded. We both took steps to leave when shouts from outside stilled us. I glanced at my second in command, a chill of warning stiffening my back.

"And so it begins." I gritted my teeth. "See that Lady Emma is protected."

Without waiting for Ewan's reply I stormed out to the courtyard. Men and women ran hither and yon, children cried and ran hand in hand with their mothers, some scooped up into their arms. Warriors called to one another, running atop the walls. The portcullis slammed shut, pinning an enemy warrior beneath it who'd made the leap over the moat onto the lifting drawing bridge.

The bastards appeared to have waited until most of our people were within the hall. What could they have hoped to gain? They were rebels, covered in filth. There was no telling how long they'd been waiting beyond the walls, hidden within the forest, biding their time.

"Archers!" I bellowed. "Take them out."

Men nocked their bows, took aim. The whistle of arrows flying, the screams beyond the wall, were a measured comfort.

"Angus." I snatched his arm as he passed me by. "Gather a crew into the boats and go to the village. Make sure the people are all right and kill anyone who stands in your way — or doesna belong here."

"Aye, my laird." Angus bellowed for a dozen of our warriors to follow and disappeared down toward the water gate.

I ran to the gate tower, taking the stairs two at a time until I reached the top. Heart pounding, I was ready for the battle to begin, as much as I was ready for it to be over. The enemy warriors were ill-prepared, and ran in the opposite direction, several of their comrades having fallen under the arrows of my men.

"Dinna let them escape!" I ordered. Arrows continued to fly, but that wasn't going to get them all. "Lower the bridge! Raise the portcullis! Ready my mount!"

I flew down the stairs, my horse at the ready and several warriors set to ride out with me.

"Not one of them is to go free," I ordered.

I didna wait for the gate to lower completely but forced my mount to race over the wooden planks and leap the rest of the way over the moat.

A few stragglers ran on foot, while three others were galloping full force on their mounts toward the woods.

"Move!" I urged my mount forward, leaning low over his neck, a bloodthirsty smile curling my lips. I loved the chase, and loved prevailing even more.

I rode past the men on foot, my targets were the men on horse. My mount's hooves pounded over the moors. Water and mud that collected from the storm flicked up all around me. The warhorse's muscles bunched and lengthened beneath me as he worked to do my bidding and with each passing second he gained on the three jackanapes who thought they might triumph over me.

But in this, there could only be one winner.

Me. The Guardian of Scotland.

I reached behind me and pulled my claymore from its scabbard, holding it in an arch behind me with both hands. My mount knew the drill. I neared the first rider and swung down, slicing through his back in one stroke. I turned to the left, arching up and swinging down once more. Second rider, down.

The third looked back, horror etched on his sorry face. There was nowhere to go. Nowhere to hide.

I snarled at him and the man faltered, shifted in his saddle and lurched to the right, falling partially out of his seat. I took the advantage, rode forward until we were parallel and then I slowed my mount and kicked the arsehole off the horse. He fell with a grunt to the ground. His horse didna stop running.

I slowed my mount to a walk and led him in a circle around the fallen man.

"Looks like ye will nay be escaping."

He looked up at me fear etched in the crinkles of his face and sweat dripping from his temples. Holding up his hands in surrender, he said, "Please, man, dinna kill me. Take me to your laird. Show mercy."

My grin only widened. "I am the laird. And mercy is what ye'll be begging for until the end of your life."

I leapt from the horse and grabbed the jackal by his nape, twirled him around, not caring about the pain I caused by wrenching up his arms. The man screamed as I pulled his shoulders into an unnatural position.

"Shut your mouth. Be a man." He whimpered as I tied his hands. "I hope ye enjoy the run."

"What?" he asked.

I tied him to the back of the horse. "Get ready to run."

His eyes widened as realization dawned on him. "No! No, please, my laird!"

"There's no use begging. I am not a merciful man."

The ride proved a bit much for the enemy warrior who'd fallen the last several hundred feet and dragged behind the horse. His plaid and shirt were covered in muck, his limbs and chin scraped. He moaned and rolled onto his back.

"My laird!" Angus ran forward, blood trickling from a gash in his forehead.

"Are ye all right?" I asked, worried for the older man.

He held up his hand. "Just fine now. But—" He shook his head, the worry in his eyes making my stomach twist.

"Tell me."

"'Tis Allan 'o the Wisp, my laird."

"What of him?" I asked, but I already had an idea of what he was going to say.

"He's gone, my laird."

"Damn." I ground my teeth. "How long?"

Angus swiped at the trickle of blood dripping into his eyebrow. "Not long. Someone broke him out. They attacked us at the water gate, took a long boat out to one of your ships."

"And my ships?" I enunciated each word.

"One is gone."

"What are ye still doing here, then?" I glanced over at my captive, languishing in the mud. "Go after my ship. I've got a prisoner to question."

CHAPTER THIRTEEN

Emma

"Leave this place." Strong arms snaked around my middle and my throat, pinning me against a strange, uninvited body. I opened my mouth to scream but no sound came out. Fear froze me. "If ye stay. I'll kill him, I swear it." The vile words were hissed into my ears.

No! I wanted to shout, to run, to elbow the asshole who'd grabbed hold of me, but I couldn't. My muscles were immobilized. This wasn't Logan playing a trick on me. Couldn't be. Not this time.

Bile curdled at the base of my tongue, and I swallowed repeatedly, even with the painful pressure on my neck.

I couldn't identify who spoke, his voice was so low. But I knew from the feel of his chest that it was a man. A warrior. And he was deadly serious.

The door to my bed chamber was within sight—Logan's, too. I'd just barely made it back from my humiliation in the great hall when the stranger leapt from nowhere and seized hold of me. I closed my eyes feeling more than stupid. I should have stayed put behind the barred door. Should have known that when Logan and his entire clan were in one room and I wasn't, that I was an easy target. But I didn't. I'd had to tell him about what I remembered.

Oh, God! What if the man holding me was an escaped prisoner? I was surely going to suffer.

"Dinna underestimate me. Ye'll wake to find him bleeding and cold beside ye."

The image was all too real and all too frightening.

There was no bluff behind his words. No reason given not to believe him. He didn't shake, tremble, nor move. He stood still as stone behind me, like being held by a carved garden statue. His tone was even, hard-edged. This was no veiled suggestion to get the hell out of dodge, this man was genuinely threatening Logan's life.

And I was scared. Terrified. I had no doubt this man would make the attempt on Logan's life. Now, if Logan knew I was fearful, he'd scoff. Boast loudly of his skills as a warrior, and I didn't disbelieve that he could fight this man off—but there was always the chance that he wouldn't. Or he could be hurt. Badly or not, there was no penicillin here if his injury became infected.

The risks were too great.

And yet the end result was me running away. I didn't want to leave Logan. There was no telling if I left this place that I would travel back in time. I'd literally be tossed into the wild on my own, a frightful situation in its own right.

But worse than all that was that I'd have to be separated from Logan.

"Do ye hesitate, bitch? Dinna ye love the man? Or do ye want to see his guts spilled at your feet?"

Somehow, I was able to force the muscles of my neck to move, pushing my head from side to side. He knew I loved Logan. He was the one spying on us. The one who shredded my lingerie, put the knife in the door. But why? I had to find out why…

"Good. Verra good." He walked forward, kicking my heels as he pushed me toward the door of my chamber. "I'll let go of one of your arms. Open the door."

The idea of using my free arm to punch him, pinch him or do some sort of damage crossed my mind, but I quickly squelched it. He still had hold of my throat and could choke the life from me.

Slowly, he slid his arm to the side allowing my arm to go free. "Open the door," he said once more.

Good lord, I had no feeling in my arm, my hand. Either from fear or from how tightly he held me, my fingers had gone numb. I forced my hand toward the door and painful prickles filled the digits all the way to their tips. Touching the cold iron of the handle stung and I recoiled.

He growled, a deep rumble that shot a spike of fear straight through my core. I jerked my hand forward, turned the handle and pushed it as far open as I could with what little leeway he'd given me.

"Inside," he ground out and shoved me inside, his tight grip letting me go and causing me to pitch forward.

I fell hard on my hands and knees, prickling limbs sending painful barbs to ricochet from end to end. I cried out, stifling the sound with a bite to my lip, afraid he'd hurt me even more for calling attention to us. The metallic tang of blood dripped into my mouth.

Lifting up onto all fours, I pushed myself to stand. My assailant blocked the doorway with his huge body. His face was covered with a black linen sack, the eyes and mouth cut out. He looked like something straight out of a nightmare. Worse than a nightmare, because he embodied everything I feared. I could feel a scream bubbling at the back of my throat and I worked hard to swallow it down, against my instincts.

"Dinna do it. Ye make a sound and I'll slit your throat, and then his." He made a motion with his hand from one side of his neck to the other.

How could he know I was about to scream? Logan often said my emotions were written on my face, and I supposed this man could read them, too. For a moment I thought that perhaps he was Logan, playing a trick on me given our last lesson. But this man was all wrong. He was thicker in the middle, shorter, legs like tree trunks.

I tamped down my scream and nodded.

If he wanted me to leave, why was he putting me in my room? Dear God, I hope he didn't plan to...

"Get your cloak and put on your boots."

I followed his instructions without thought, sitting on the edge of my bed to lace my boots with trembling fingers. I held my sobs in check, very close to breaking down.

"I'm going to leave ye now. But I trust ye'll leave Gealach right behind me."

"Why?" I asked.

He let out short, brutal laugh. "Dinna ask questions ye dinna want the answers to."

His answer confused me, but I nodded all the same, feeling dejected, miserable, scared. There was nothing more I could do. I would not be the cause of Logan's death. The idea of departing left me feeling soulless. I didn't belong here and I never had — except when I was alone with Logan. But the choice was no longer mine. It'd been stripped from me by the vile asshole standing in my doorway.

My heart squeezed painfully. The bastard crushed it figuratively with his demands.

My fingers faulted on the laces. The waffling I'd done, not telling Logan the truth... God, why hadn't I told him? At least then when he found me missing he would have just assumed I'd gone back to my own time. Now I feared he'd never stop looking for me. Even gone, I was going to be a burden to him. We'd reached a place, I thought, where we understood each other. He loved me and I loved him, it was obvious — though his behavior in the great hall confused me, I understood it.

A note at least... Something.

"If ye're not gone within a quarter hour, I'll give the signal and Grant dies."

I swallowed back the bile that took residence in my throat. Nodding once more, I couldn't find the words to speak. My voice was...gone, just as my heart turned to ash. I knew, deep down, I'd never love another like I did Logan. It was magical. Endless. Infinite.

And leaving him...leaving what we had was—

Soul crushing.

There was a circle of stones atop a nearby ridge. I didn't know which one, and I wouldn't have much time to get there, but it was my only hope for returning to my time, and saving Logan. I couldn't stay here, not in this era. Not if I couldn't have him.

If I was going to be forced to start anew, I was going to start in a place where there was no turning back at a moment of weakness. A moment that could destroy everything and kill Logan.

But I had to leave a clue for him. Some sort of message that let him know I was gone forever.

I stood from the bed which was completely made. This room held a lot more sentimentality for me than I'd previously thought. I was going to miss it. Miss everything about it. Tears burned my eyes, welling so that my vision blurred. I didn't want to leave. As much as I'd thought about it before, when it came down to it. I didn't want to.

The door closed and I whirled around to see that my assailant was gone. Fifteen minutes. That was all I had to get away from here.

My stomach flipped, and I doubled over, worried for a moment I might vomit. Being with Logan gave me such strength. I associated my change—my confidence, my whole persona on life—with him. How was I going to be able to survive without him?

I stood up straight. Swiped angrily at the tears cooling tracks on my cheeks. I had to survive, to adapt to life without him. I just had to. There was no other choice. The truth was, that while Logan had shown me there was some strength within me, I was the one in control of my life. And yes, my heart was breaking, but I was also saving him.

I glanced around the room, looking for something I could leave behind as a message not to come looking for me.

The ring.

I glanced down at my right ring finger where the gold band with a shell from Gealach's beach rested. The ring that Logan gave me just a few weeks prior. A token I would have wanted to take with me, to cherish forever. I slipped it from my finger and rested in on my pillow, took a step back and then snatched it up again.

I had to leave it. But he'd never find it on my pillow. What if it fell? Or Agatha didn't see it when she turned down my blankets?

Curling my fingers around the ring, I closed my eyes, swallowing hard and working harder to bottle up all the emotions taking over.

Probably only twelve or thirteen minutes now.

I wrenched the ribbon from my hair and secured it around the ring, and then tied it to the post so it dangled, ironically in front of the carvings of a sheep nuzzling a wildcat.

There was nothing more to do, except get the hell out before the madman decided to take Logan's life in his hands. I practically ran from the room. My strides were long down the hall, fingers curled tightly into my skirts. I took the back stairs until I reached the entrance to the water gate. The guards looked at me like I might be crazy. And I was.

"Good afternoon," I started, fidgeting.

"My lady," they grumbled.

"I know this may seem very…unusual, but I've need to get down to the beach. I'd like to…take a walk." And then from there, escape to the ridge.

The guards frowned, but only one spoke. "I dinna think the laird would approve."

"Oh, but you see, he doesn't know. It's a surprise. I wanted to find a shell for him, to make him a necklace. A gift for good luck."

The men looked at each other and didn't speak for several seconds that felt interminable. Precious seconds that ticked by and nearly threw me into hysterics. Five minutes tops was all I had left.

"Fine then, but ye'll need an escort."

Time for feminine wiles, not something I'd ever been that great at. I reached out, touched his forearm where his leather bracer was tied to ward off any stray blows. "Oh, please, I must hurry. I want to give it to him tonight. I promise, if I run into trouble, I'll call for help."

The man frowned, and I swore if he didn't make up his mind in the next ten seconds—

"Ye've got a few minutes. Nothing more, else 'tis our heads."

"Oh, thank you! I promise!"

Only a few minutes to escape.

I walked down the stairs to the water's edge, my foot sinking into the sand. I turned and waved goodbye, walked slowly until I turned and the stone walls of the cave took me out of sight. And then I ran.

Ran like the devil was about to bite my ass. I ran so hard my muscles screamed and my lungs long since stopped working. I ran until I wanted to puke and thought I'd surely die of a heart attack. And when I could no longer push myself with thoughts of Logan dying, I collapsed just inside the woods at the base of a ridge. Hopefully the right ridge.

I only allowed myself a minute of rest. By now the guards would have alerted Logan that I'd left, and he would have found my ring if he dared to check in our room first. I should have found another way to escape. But there was no time, and no other way that I could think of. Walking out the front gate would never have worked.

Pushing to my feet, I trudged with legs that were going numb, up the side of the ridge. My hands stung from catching myself numerous times when I fell. Sweat slicked over my skin, and I would have given anything for a glass of cold water. What felt like hours later, I finally reached the top of the ridge, and a circle of stones stood proud and oddly tranquil in its center. Trees ringed the outside, as if even they didn't dare grow in the middle.

I started to shake. I don't know if it was fear or nerves or just having endured the most excruciating marathon of my life, but I trembled all the same and my teeth chattered.

Time to move forward. If I was going to disappear I needed it to happen now. Not when I had the chance to change my mind, or when Logan happened to find me.

I stepped between two of the stones, already feeling power emanate from their thickness and flow through my body. I leaned against one, hoping it would give me strength to do what I needed to do and step into the middle. It was cool against the raging heat of my body. Sweat fairly poured from my exertive run. I didn't think I could take another step. Not without help from the magical stones.

Miraculously, my feet moved, and overhead a rumble of thunder sounded. A chill stole over me. I was doing the right thing. The storm was a clue.

Fate wanted this. And that gave me strength to move forward. One foot in front of the other.

I found the center. Stood with arms out and looked up to the sky, half-expecting a bolt of lightning to come down and strike me right in the chest. Dark clouds circled above, fraught with lines of white as lightning struck its center. All I had to do was wait for something magical to happen. It was bound to occur.

I closed my eyes. "Take me home," I whispered to the divine. "Take me back."

The thunder grew louder and a swift wind blew, taking my loose hair up in its arms and whipping it around. Chills covered me. A few drops of rain dripped coolly on my cheeks, sliding down over the line of my jaw to my neck, taking away the heat of my skin, and replacing it within a sense of being refreshed, relaxed. "Yes. Take me where I belong," I murmured, hoping my encouragement would ease my passage back into the future.

But nothing happened. The wind stopped. Rain no longer fell. Thunder silenced and the sun covered my cheeks. I was still here. I'd not gone back home. If anything, I felt a stronger pull to Gealach and the land.

"No!" I cried. "Oh, Logan." I crumbled, my knees hitting the ground and beat my fists into the soft, grassy ground. "Why have you decided I belong here? He's going to die."

"I willna die, Emma. But I might beat ye to death for what ye've put me through." Logan's voice sliced through my sobs, and I jerked my gaze up, choking on a gasp.

He stood on the outside of the circle, arms crossed over his massive chest and a glower on his face that should have sent me running straight for the cliff's edge, but it only brought me a great sense of relief.

"Logan. You're alive." I shook my head, sadness filling me. "You shouldn't have come here."

CHAPTER FOURTEEN

Logan

Emma looked devastated, kneeling there in the grass. Her eyes were red and puffy. Cheeks blotchy from crying. Her lower lip quivered, and her hands trembled as she touched them to her cheeks. Emma shook her head as if disbelieving her own eyes.

"You need to go back. You need to leave me here." She looked away, frantically searching the woods surrounding us.

I was surprised she was more fearful of what was on the outside of the stone circle then of me.

"Explain yourself," I managed to say. I kept my feet rooted in place for fear I'd charge into the circle and shake her until her head rolled from side to side.

Fire filled my blood. If I opened my mouth too wide, I was sure to breathe flames like the mighty dragon I felt like. Hearing my death on her lips was shocking, unspeakable, and filled me with rage and, oddly, curiosity.

"I...I can't." She stood, still shaking her head as though she couldn't wrap her mind around the situation we found ourselves in.

The lass was run ragged. Her hair flew in all different directions. Her gown was torn, mud coated the hem and streaks of muck ran down her skirts. A smear crossed her nose and forehead. Emma needed a bath, but I still found her utterly enchanting in her unkempt state.

I took a step forward but stopped when energy charged through my limbs, seeming to come from the ground itself. Was it my imagination? My anger? Or did this circle of stones hold some unexplainable power over the both of us? The circle was a sacred place, I knew that and didna disrespect it for what it was. But to send a rush through my leg? Now I was the one shaking my head. I crossed my arms over my chest and willed the tingly sensations to leave my limbs.

"I'm nay asking ye, Emma. Tell me. Now."

She glanced up at me, fear vivid in her eyes. "Didn't you find the ring?"

"The ring?" I shook my head, not understanding what the hell a piece of jewelry had to do with anything.

Emma glanced behind me as though in a panic. "I left the ring tied to the bed post. Hoped you would understand."

"Ye're speaking nonsense, I dinna understand ye." I roved my gaze over her. She shook. Fear filled her face. "Emma, I was merely teasing when I said I'd beat yet to death. I'll nay harm ye, I promise."

Her eyes widened and she frowned. "I wasn't speaking about that! You aren't the one I'm afraid of." She slapped a hand over her mouth, and large tears spilled over her cheeks and fingers, making streaks in the grime.

"Who has scared ye. I'll take care of them, I swear it."

Whoever put this fear in her would feel it on the rack and as I slowly ripped them apart and they bled in a pool of their own blood. I'd make sure of it.

"Oh, Logan!" She ran toward me then, threw herself in my arms. I gripped onto her tight, buried my face in her hair. We'd come so close to her disappearing from my life. I couldn't imagine a life without her. "They will kill you, and it's all my fault."

"What are ye talking about?" I wanted to ask why she thought herself to be at fault, but didna dare, not yet anyway. Was she trying to tell me that after all this time, all we'd shared she was in truth my enemy?

She trembled and held onto me tighter. "He came to me, grabbed me..."

"Who?" A murderous rage burned deep within me. I clenched my teeth so tight pain seared through my jaw.

"A masked man. He said he'd kill you if I didn't leave right away."

"Gealach?"

She nodded, wiping tears on my shoulder, soaking the *leine* through.

Who could want her to leave Gealach? What power did she hold? Were the threats all along someone's hopes that she would leave? What sense did it make?

"He said he'd kill you. And he will."

"Hush now, lass. No one is going to kill me. Many have tried, none have succeeded."

Emma tried to push away from me, shaking her head. I wouldn't let her go. Couldn't. She stopped fighting and instead clutched at my chest.

"There is more than one. He mentioned another. All it would take was one signal from him and they'd come after you." Emma's trembling subsided a little.

I stroked her wild hair, smoothing it down her back. "Ye needn't worry, love. I will nay let anyone harm me, nor ye. I mean to kill the bastard."

"How will you know who he is?" She pulled her face from my shoulder and looked up at me, fear shining bright in her eyes. "I wouldn't be able to tell you."

"Certainly there was something you could have noticed about him?"

She glanced away, bit her lip as though trying to drum up from the recesses of her mind some unseen clue. "Only his size. He wore a black mask that covered his entire face. And I never saw who his partner was. There's no telling if there is more than just the two of them, either. I have to leave, and you need to go back."

I gripped her shoulders, gazed directly into her eyes, and spoke with authority. "Ye will not leave. Ye're coming back to Gealach with me."

"I can't." She pushed away, stepped back into the center of the stones and stared toward the sky. "I won't."

I couldna help it. Suspicion grew within me, coiling like a serpent ready to strike. "What are ye doing here, in the circle of stones?"

Emma swallowed, looked behind her, looked down at her hands smudged with dirt and a few bits of grass. "Praying," she said. "Praying to go home."

"Ye are home," I growled.

Her lips trembled all the more. She wrung her hands in front of her. "So it would seem."

An odd mixture of rage and relief filled me. How could she want to run away, and only when someone threatened my life? Did she not realize whoever the coward was, he couldna hurt me?

"Emma, I'll not allow anyone to take ye away from me."

She shook her head, denying me that claim. "You see, that's just it. I know you will try. I know that most of the time you will probably be successful, but you can't deny that you are human. There will come a time when even you can't run from your enemies. They could poison their weapons, or slice you in just the right spot that drains you of all blood."

"But now is not that time." I stood straighter, taller. If she was going to let her fear control her, than I had to be the steady hand that guided her home. I reached out, gripped her arm and pulled her against me.

"How did you find me?" she asked breathlessly.

"I will always find ye." I pressed her hand to my heart. "Ye are here within me, Emma. Always."

I wanted to punish her. Punish her for leaving me without question, for putting herself in danger—for only God and the Devil knew how many enemy warriors enclosed on us now upon the ridge.

"Dinna ever leave me again. When someone threatens ye, find me. Even if they swear to cut me down if ye do. They only seek to put fear inside ye, to weaken me through ye."

"I'm not sure that is a promise I can make."

I wanted to kiss her and thrash her at the same time. Frustration and desire warred within me. I tightened my hold on her.

"Swear it."

She shook her head, looked down at my chest. "I can't! If I were to leave again in the future it would only make me a liar."

"Damn ye, Emma, promise me." I took hold of her chin and forced her to look up at me. Her skin was warm beneath my fingertips, and yet she trembled. Her blue eyes shimmered and her ruby lips begged to be kissed. "We are as one."

"If only," she whispered, closing her eyes but not before two large tears dripped.

But I couldn't listen to her words of denial any longer. I pressed my lips to hers, taking in her sweet taste and warmth. Emma resisted, pushing against me, murmuring something about how she wouldn't be the death of me. Damn myself, for having ever told her such. I slipped my tongue beneath the crease of her lips, over her tightly shut teeth, until she relented, at least sinking against me and willingly opening herself up to my exploration.

Victory was sweet sin.

I delved inside the delicious cavern of her mouth, sipping from her kiss like a dying man would take in water over his parched lips from a river. I wanted her to know she was mine. To know that I would never let her go. I wrapped my arms around her, pulling her flush against me. Her soft curves a temptation for any man, but a potent potion to me. One drop of her affection left me forever pining after her. I could never let her know how much she affected me, and yet I was sure in my hold of her, my kiss, she would see it and know it for what it was.

Love. Sweet, tender, powerful, all-consuming love.

I lifted her off her feet, holding her in the air against me, so she couldn't get away and so I could hold her closer. Every soft curve of her form melted along the equally hard planes of my body. Emma draped her arms around my neck, clinging to me just as I clung to her. Maddening desire took me in its strangle hold. My cock pressed hard and hot against her, having no fear in telling what I wanted.

What madness it was, kissing her like this in the circle of stones. Out in the middle of the wilderness where anyone could happen upon us. One might say I taunted death, if they didna know how very much I wanted to live. But, I swore it, if Emma ever left me... Death might be my only consolation, the only peace I might ever find.

"I canna lose ye," I said, against her kiss-plumped lips.

"Oh, Logan." She touched her hand to my cheek. "I never want to lose you either... But what of —"

"Dinna speak of it. I'll take care of it. Ye have my word."

"I believe you, but —"

"Shh..." I pressed my finger to her lips. "There is no time for *but*, love."

"We have to be prepared."

I pressed my forehead to hers. "I'm always prepared for the worst. But with ye, for the times we are together, I can believe there is something better in this world."

Emma sighed, touched her lips to mine. "Me, too."

A movement beyond the circle caught my attention. A warrior, not of my clan, crept stealthily from tree to tree. But not just one, suddenly there were more of them. I didna recognize them as members of any of our allied clans. Strangers. Enemies.

"Dear God," I whispered. "Dinna move, love. We are no longer alone."

I pulled my claymore free and pushed Emma to my back.

"Remember what I told ye."

"Yes," she replied, though I was so vague I could have been reminding her of anything.

A half dozen, a dozen more. They surrounded us. I could take on five, six warriors, more if they'd no skill. But these numbers... I felt the chill of dread deep in my bones. We were far away from our castle and there were no reinforcements at our backs.

I was within their sight, and though an eerie mist had grown round our feet, if I could see them trying to hide, surely they could see me standing still inside the circle of stones. But... it didna appear that they did.

They all stared toward the stones, made signs of the cross over their chests and then kept on moving. Not one called out to me, walked toward us, made a threat. Nothing.

Almost like they saw right through us. But how could it be possible? Were we not the target, but the castle, and they believing that two lovers within a sacred circle were nay worth it?

Well, I couldna stand by while the enemy walked on my lands, without knowing their purpose. I took a step toward them.

"No, don't!" Emma whispered urgently. She gripped onto my shoulders. "Please don't."

I was torn between duty to Gealach and duty to Emma. A coward would let the warriors go, let them deal with Gealach and be on my way. But I wasn't a coward. Could never be, and despite my love for Emma, I wasn't going to let my people, my legacy, my king, suffer for that small part of me that longed to be a coward and to escape my fate.

I wouldn't be the only one that had to sacrifice love for country — and hate myself for having chosen it.

"I have no choice."

"You told me once, we all have a choice." There was a undertone of anger in her voice.

"That I did." I gripped the handle of my claymore tighter, fist over fist, pressed my lips firmly together and refused to let myself give in. I had to protect my people.

"And you…you've made another choice. A foolish one."

"Emma, mark my words, I guard our future. The choice to protect my castle — that is choosing us, though you may not realize it now."

"But they, for whatever reason, magic maybe, they can't see us."

"We are protected by the stones. Ye're right." I turned a moment and kissed her deeply. "Stay here where ye'll be safe."

A gasp, followed by a sob, escaped her. "Please, don't. Stay with me."

"That is precisely what I'm doing, lass."

And indeed, Fate did intervene. A battle cry sounded from within the forest, and suddenly Ewan appeared, fighting like a caged bear, he took down two men and then another. Behind him more Grant warriors sounded their calls, slicing, fighting, and taking the enemy apart.

I let out my own battle cry and leapt from the safety of the stone circle into the fray. My men did not appear surprised to see me, though my enemy was. Within minutes it was over, and dozens of my enemy lay dead at our feet.

"MacDonald's men," I said through bared teeth to Ewan who nodded. "How did ye know?"

"The guards told us they'd sent ye up the ridge to fetch the lady. We followed just to be sure ye were safe, and then caught the movement." He glanced around the woods. "Where is Lady Emma?"

"In the circle." I could see her clearly watching me, her face pale and eyes wide.

"I dinna understand. The circle is empty." Ewan looked just as confused as I felt.

"She is protected by Fate."

"Come to think of it, we did not see ye either, my laird."

'Twas magic, but I'd not tell Ewan that. "I must get her. Bring her back to the castle."

"Aye, we will wait."

I nodded. "It may prove to be a challenge convincing her. She's got it into her head she should leave our lands for my own good."

"An honorable lady."

"But she's wrong."

"Aye."

"Ye agree?" I looked sharply at Ewan.

"'Tis true ye've not been the same since Lady Emma graced the halls of Gealach, but ye've also been much improved. 'Tis a change we are all grateful for, my laird."

I was stunned at the revelation, and relieved. "Nod if ye see me enter the circle. Shake your head if nay."

"My laird?"

"Just do it," I ordered. I'd a need raging through me to claim what was mine within the circle, and I'd just as rather not do it with all my men watching. What better place to make Emma mine forever than within the sacred stones that made us each other's fates?

"Aye, my laird."

I walked with slow, determined purpose up toward the circle. Emma's gaze was steadily on mine and she licked her lips, a nervous habit, I gathered.

"Thank God you weren't hurt," she said.

"Foolish warriors. Dinna fash, lass."

Still, her hand was at her throat and she looked ready to run, scream or toss up her last meal. "I was so scared."

"I'm here now."

"Yes."

I turned around to find Ewan staring with disbelief at the circle. He kept shaking his head and looking around. He couldna see us, and yet he called his men to stand at attention, turning their backs from the circle to stand watch.

"They canna see us, Emma."

"What?" She crept up beside me and gazed at the warriors.

"The stones are protecting us. 'Tis the reason why the enemy crept past us, seemingly without a care for our presence."

"We are invisible?"

"To the outside world."

"What does it mean?"

"I think it means exactly what ye believe." I took Emma's hands in mine and held them to my chest. "What were ye hoping to accomplish when ye came here?"

"To Gealach?"

I shook my head. "Nay, to the stone circle."

"I was hoping that…"

"Magic would take ye to where ye belong?"

"Yes… Anywhere, but where you were. I didn't want to put you in harm's way."

"I know it, and I'll not blame ye for it. But dinna ye see? Ye are still here. *This* is where ye belong. With me. And the Gods or Fate or Destiny, wants us to be together."

"But you said yourself it was too dangerous and I couldn't—" Her voice broke.

"Ye can, and we will." I kissed her then, silencing her denial. "I want to make love to ye here, in this sacred place."

"We can't!" She glanced at the warriors. "Not with all of them a dozen feet away."

"They canna hear us or see us." I tugged her closer. "Feel what ye do to me. I want ye. I want ye, now."

I pressed my cock, hard as stone and aching for the sheath of her warm, wet cunt, to the apex of her thighs. The heat of her body seeped between our clothes, cradling me in its illustrious temptation. Emma sighed, tucking her hips forward in silent acceptance.

"I feel like we're in some ancient ritual, having sex in the middle of sacred stones for all the world to see," she whispered.

"Think of it as the two of us binding ourselves to one another. Giving in to what the Gods, and what we, want."

"I do want you. I…" She swallowed, her words sucked back inside her.

I knew what she wanted to say, could see the words fairly spelled on her breath. She loved me. And I her. Why was it so hard for us to speak the words?

"Ye are my future," I said. But when she opened her lips to respond, I claimed them in a savage kiss.

Discovering what Fate had designed for us, having fought a battle and won, having not yet defeated our enemies that lurked with the place we thought we were safe...that was all enough for one moment.

"Let us give our consciousness over to passion. No more words or fears. Just us. Just peace and pleasure," I said.

Emma nodded, gripping the buckle of my belt and tugging. We stripped each other in a frenzy, standing nude, our feet barely visible in the mist, droplets of moisture making Emma's and my own skin glow as though we'd been sprinkled with fae dust.

She wrapped her hands around my cock, stroking up and down in way that stole my breath. My head fell back, but I forced it forward so I could gaze into her eyes. She stared up at me boldly, the heated seductress returned.

Emma lowered to her knees, her lips parallel to my shaft. I threaded my hands through her hair, wanting more than anything for her to suck me deep into her velvet mouth. She teased me, flexing and unflexing her hand, breathing hotly on my oversensitive flesh.

"Do it," I commanded, though in truth I was begging.

"This?" The tip of her pink tongue flicked out, skimming over the ridge of my cock head, then along the vein that throbbed over the top of my length.

"Aye. That." I hissed a breath. "I love when ye tease me."

"Mmm." She was a siren, a sensual wraith come to steal my soul, and as her perfect tongue flicked and teased over my cock, I was ready to give it up. To give her anything she wanted, now and forever.

And then she sucked me deep. Fingers curling around my sac as she massaged me with both her hands and her tongue. My cock touched the back of her throat and still she sucked me deeper, as though she'd swallow me whole. I was not a man who admitted that his knees could grow weak, but shaky they were. I locked them tight, jutting my hips forward in time with the bob of her mouth.

"*Mo creach*," I moaned.

She slowed her movements, taking me into her mouth inch by torturous inch, and then back out, sucking the head and swirling her tongue over it, dipping into the center. Chills covered my entire body, and I tightened every muscle to keep from trembling. Held my breath until my lungs burst with the need for air.

I couldna allow her to continue, unless I, too, was giving her pleasure. "Stand up," I demanded.

She shook her head.

"Now."

Emma pulled back a look of confusion on her face. I pulled her in for a hot, demanding kiss, crushing her lips to mine. But I broke that off abruptly, too, prepared to wrap her legs around me and thrust home. But that wasn't the way this was going to go. Not yet.

"Turn around."

Emma did as I said without question.

"Bend over and touch your hands to the ground."

Again, she listened, and dear Lord did I get the view of every man's fantasy. Ripe, plump rear, slick, pink cunt.

I slapped her buttocks, one side and then the other, and she whimpered.

"That was for running away," I said, smoothing my hand over the reddened cheeks. "But this is for coming back with me."

Bracing my legs apart to keep balance, I lifted her legs into the air, so she stood on her hands, then laid them on my shoulders, and gripping her about the waist, brought her up into the air, so her dew-drenched sex was within an inch of my mouth and my cock prodded along her plump, inviting lips.

Emma shrieked and grabbed hold of my thighs. "What are you doing?"

I chuckled, grinning at both her reaction and the sweet treat I was about to receive.

"Shocking ye, lass."

"I've never even imagined—" Before she could finish a word, I ducked between her thighs, sliding my tongue along the glistening folds. The next sound from her mouth was a luscious moan.

Within seconds, Emma took my cock back into her mouth and the two of us feasted on each other. I took a few careful steps back so I could lean against one of the stones for support. There was only so much I could handle. My muscles shook from pleasure, from the desire to burst into her sweet mouth, and from the need to keep myself from doing so.

Emma's legs trembled, and I smoothed a hand up over her hip to massage her soft, rounded buttocks. I could nestle between her thighs for days, weeks, months. Live off of her essence alone, so sweet and tangy.

With her pleasuring me while I pleasured her, it was a feat in itself to keep myself from exploding. Every time I thought about our position, where we were, what I was doing, and listening to each sweet little moan vibrating against my cock, it was more than I—

Jolts of lightning shot across my spine. I was close. So damn close.

I mouthed her clit, suckling gently, and then pulling away. Teasing her like she taunted me. We were both on the precipice of climax, dangling over the edge, waiting for the other to grab hold. But I refused to finish until she did.

"Let go, my love," I said, stroking her folds with the rough stubble of my chin before pressing my lips hotly against the bundle of tense, pleasure-filled nerves.

Emma moaned louder, sucked harder. Her fingers dug into the backs of my thighs. Not even a second passed before she was crying out, her thighs clamping against my face. I groaned loudly, bucking my hips forward as my own release took hold, and God bless her, she sucked in every last drop.

We stood motionless for a moment, until I worried so much blood could have rushed to her head by now that she'd have lost consciousness. I cradled her in my arms and laid her on the ground, sliding down beside her.

"Ye didna fall asleep," I murmured, swirling fingers over her puckered nipples. She shivered, and sucked in a breath.

"How could I?"

I chuckled and traced a finger over her cheek. "I was afraid all the blood would rush from your heart to your head."

Emma smiled and kissed me briefly. "That would not have been any fun."

"Nay. No fun at all."

My men still stood watch, and I knew they would for days to come if I commanded it. But, with their safety in mind, and ours, it was time for us to return to Gealach.

"We must dress and get ye safely behind the walls again."

Emma raised her brows, and I could practically hear her thoughts.

"I will ensure your attacker is found and taken to the dungeon."

"And his partner."

"Aye."

"How?"

"Easy. If they aim to kill me, then what better way to do it then announce ye haven't gone any place."

Emma shook her head, jumped to her feet and held her gown in front of her beautiful body, hiding it from my view. She shook her head vehemently.

I tugged at the hem of her gown. "Ye mustn't worry, love. I will nay be harmed."

"How can you be sure? He's a madman!"

"And who says I'm not?"

CHAPTER FIFTEEN

Emma

Cheers cracked the silence of the Highland wilds as our horses crossed the heath toward the castle. The gates were lowered and hundreds stood in wait of our return. It seemed only natural that Logan's people would be joyful at seeing him, but they cheered just as much for me. I was stunned by it.

The uproar at our return was only overshadowed by the turmoil our departure seemed to have wreaked on Gealach. The servants ran about as though they'd forgotten the jobs they'd done for years, and even the warriors seemed out of sorts — though a few quick orders from Logan, followed by Ewan, seemed to put them back to rights.

To say I was shocked would be an understatement. I was completely at a loss for words. They actually *cared* about me?

Logan held me in his arms atop his horse, and I felt just as safe in his warm embrace as I did behind the stone walls. The men who'd fought with him up on the ridge also proudly sat on their mounts. A mean looking brood they were, armed to the teeth, but I knew they were all Logan's best men, and they fought with heart, and served their laird with passion.

Agatha nearly brought me to tears when I saw her. The stern older woman's eyes watered. Normally put together, her grey hair had come a little loose from her bun, and the hem of her usually pristine plaid was smudged. Agatha took pride in her position within the house. Hated to look unkempt, and yet here she was, completely bedraggled. Had she been looking for me too? She clutched my ring in her hands.

Logan dismounted, then reached up, wrapping his hands around my waist as he brought me down. A brief, secret smile touched his lips.

"Shall I have a bath drawn?" Agatha managed to say, though her voice cracked.

Distracted away from Logan, I said, "Yes, please. I could use one." I was covered in a film of sweat from running and making love.

My stomach growled. Agatha perked up, swiped at the tears in her eyes.

"Should ye like a bite to eat as well, my lady?"

I shook my head, glancing at Logan, and trying hard not to smile. After all, we didn't need to be completely on display. "I plan to attend dinner this evening in the great hall with the laird. And I'm afraid if I eat anything now, I won't be hungry when dinner arrives."

Agatha raised her brow and opened her mouth to speak, but Logan chimed in. "A small bite willna hurt. After all, ye had plenty of exercise today."

I felt a blush creep from my chest, up over my cheeks. No one in the house had any idea what went on today—other than I'd disappeared and the laird went after me. I'm sure our behavior now was more confusing than ever. It came natural to act so in love, even though we'd tried to hide it for months. After the culprits were imprisoned, would Logan keep up the pretense of his fondness in public or sequester us back to the darkness of our rooms?

"All right. Will you join me?" I was pushing it, I knew. But I couldn't help myself. I wanted Logan in my bath with me, feeding me whatever snack from his fingertips and licking droplets of wine from my flesh.

"I wish I could, my lady, but I'm afraid I willna be seeing ye until the evening meal." He winked before turning away and giving orders to his housekeeper and steward about the evening. Then he leaned back toward me and whispered. "Ye're doing very well. Bar the door when ye get to your room. I'll have guards posted."

Before I had the chance to reply, he summoned two guards to escort me to my room. Dear God, I hoped neither of them were against Logan. No doubt he'd already thought about that.

One guard stood beside me in the hallway while the other searched my room. Appearing to find no one there ready to attack me, he let me in.

"Bar the door, my lady."

I nodded. "Thank you."

I closed the door and put the bar in place. I sat on the edge of the bed and waited. Only a few minutes would go by before I needed to open the door once more for Agatha and my bath. A steady stream of servants would come in. Any one of them with a knife hidden up their sleeve.

And what was now happening with Logan? Was an arrow lodged in his heart? A knife pressed at his jugular? I closed my eyes, finding it hard to swallow past the lump in my throat. I'd brought danger on him. Had willingly come back to be a part of this insane charade. And why? Because he asked me to. What was I thinking, agreeing for him to be bait?

Hoping to get my mind off my fear I stared at the bed posts, trying to decipher exactly what each design could mean. I'd not noticed before, but there, positioned almost like a halo, was a Celtic rune above the head of a lion. It looked just like the one on my hip. The one that Logan said meant we were destined for each other. And here it was, carved into the wood, just as it was carved onto my flesh.

Perhaps there was more to our story than met the eye. More than either of us had any control over.

What did it matter when I had no idea what was happening downstairs—or wherever Logan was?

A swift knock at the door and Agatha's call on the other side had me jumping from the bed and swiping at tears I'd not realized were falling. I took the bar down as fast as I could and opened the door to her and a slew of servants. The servants glanced at me from the sides of their eyes as they went about their work, making me feel completely uncomfortable. I shifted on my feet waiting, and at last, they left and only Agatha remained.

"What is his lairdship doing?" I asked. It was completely out of place to ask. I knew I shouldn't, and yet I couldn't hold back.

"Well, I suspect he's getting a bath, too."

"A bath?" Logan preferred swimming in the loch.

"Aye. I saw a bath go in just as I brought this one in here."

I almost said, *ah*, aloud. This was the closest way for us both to bathe together, without sharing a tub. I stared at the closed door between our two rooms and Agatha must have followed my line of vision, because she clucked her tongue and tugged me around.

"Mustn't get excited about the laird in his bath, my lady."

I wanted to ask why not. Agatha knew plenty what I was to Logan, and what he was to me. I allowed her to undress me, sink me into the steamy water, and soap my hair until my scalp stung with freshness. The film of sweat and fear was sluiced off my tingling skin with a soft sponge and lemon-scented soap. By the time I was dressed, my hair dried before a fire and elegantly twisted into a bun, with curled tendrils at my temples, I felt more like myself.

Well, the girl that traveled back in time five-hundred years and made love to a Highland warrior in the center of a sacred circle of stones.

"I believe ye left this behind today." Agatha pressed my ring into my hands and gave me an odd look.

I stared at the ring in the center of my palm—avoiding her questioning gaze. "Thank you." I didn't want to give in to her curiosity. To tell her I'd run away, only to be back again. To tell her I'd put her master's life in danger, as well as her own. She'd never forgive me, and I didn't think at that moment I could handle one more thing to worry over. I slipped the ring onto my finger. A treasure I was so very glad to have returned.

"Well, then, ye have it back." She held her hand toward the small table by my hearth. "I brought ye a wee bit to eat. Just an apple and a delicious nut butter that Cook has been experimenting with."

My eyes widened. Was it possible? Truly?

I rushed to the table to see the apple sliced thinly and a dollop of what looked to be all natural almond butter. At least the way it looked in the jar, crunchy and smooth at the same time.

"What type of nuts?" I picked up an apple and a dab of the butter.

"Almond, my lady."

"My favorite." I took a bite, the blend of crispy, sweet fruit with the richness of the almond butter was enough to make me audibly sigh. "Delicious."

"I'll tell Cook ye think so."

"Yes, please do. I'd be happy to have this for my snack every day."

A short time later, I descended into the great hall with Logan by my side. Behind us stood four guards and in front of us another two. Logan wasn't taking any chances, obviously.

Once inside the great hall, members of the Grant clan stood, bowing their heads as Logan passed, and I couldn't help feeling a little like I'd been put on the spot. Until this very moment, I'd been kept out of sight. Clan members were only told that I was a guest, not their laird's…lover. And now, I walked on his arm down the center of two large trestle tables toward the head table like a bride at her wedding. Except there was one very big difference—Logan and I were not married, nor had there ever been any talk of marriage.

Oh, what would they think of me? Would their opinion of me sink because I was… No, I was not his mistress. And even if I was, there were plenty of mistresses in history who'd been given the respect of the people. Weren't there? A sinking dread stewed in the pit of my belly. Not really.

I kept my shoulders straight, chin up, trying for brave, when despite how I felt there were worse things to be worried over than what the people thought of me. For one, an archer could have his arrow aimed at Logan at that very moment. Or worse tonight's meal was poisoned, and he would unsuspectingly bite into it, falling dead on his plate.

"Dinna fash yourself, lass." Logan spoke in low tones and patted my hand resting on his arm and giving me a gentle squeeze. "They willna bite."

But they might kill him. "Do you have a food tester?"

Logan chuckled. "I will not be poisoned."

I managed a smile and nodded, trying my best to believe he would know. "Who do they think I am?"

Maybe it was me that was going to end up poisoned. Whoever the culprit was believed me to be a whore who deserved no better.

"My guest. I've told them that many times."

"And yet, this night seems…"

"Different?"

"Yes."

"I think that's because 'tis different for the both of us. No one else knows what happened today…in the center of the stones."

It was hard to keep the gasp inside, but I did all the same, not wanting anyone to sense the way his words or the images he brought up made my entire body light on fire. If he'd even hinted at it, I would have turned around and run straight back to that stone circle, one of our bedrooms or even the closest alcove, lifted my gown and begged for him to pleasure me.

"Tonight, we need to be each other's strength," he murmured before pulling a chair out for me at the table. The scraping of the wood startled me and I jumped.

"Ye must relax," he said in low tones.

I took a seat and let him tuck me in. "I will try."

"Ye will succeed."

I was glad at least he had confidence in our situation. I dared a glance upward to see the entire dining hall facing us, as though waiting for something. Candlelight flickered in their eyes and off their curious faces.

"We give thanks today for this bountiful feast," Logan said to the crowd, lifting his mug into the air. "And to our continued safety."

There was a great cheer from the crowd before they took their seats and food piled high upon platters was eagerly dug into.

"Is today a special occasion?" I fingered the silverware on either side of my plate. I got the feeling that not every meal was like this.

Logan plopped a great deal of succulent meat onto my plate and then drizzled a red sauce over it. "Indeed, Emma, 'tis."

I speared a piece and contemplated its coloring, deciding it must be pork. "What is the occasion?"

Logan took a deep breath. When he spoke, there was sadness in his voice. "'Tis the anniversary of my father's death. And my birthday."

"Oh!" I gasped and turned to face him. "Why didn't you tell me?" I couldn't imagine how it felt to celebrate the day of your birth along with someone so dear's death. And I'd not been able to give him a present.

"I dinna make a big fuss over it."

"But this celebration?"

"The clan's doing. And appropriate timing, dinna ye think?"

I nodded, biting my lip. "I'm afraid I don't—" But before I could tell him I didn't have a present for him, commotion broke out at the entrance to the great hall.

Logan shoved back in his chair, toppling it as he stood, and drew his sword. "Explain yourselves."

Two men were brought struggling into the hall, cursing and kicking the guards who roughly handled them. These had to be the two. One had the same thick, trunk-like legs, and appeared to be of identical build to the man who accosted me.

Logan glanced down at me and I nodded.

Having confirmed that I recognized the man, in a move straight from an action movie, Logan leapt onto the table before jumping to the floor and strode toward the captured men with vengeful steps.

When he reached the men, he grabbed the larger one by his shirt and pulled him forward. I leaned closer to the table, hoping to catch a whisper of what he said. Whatever he said was enough to make both men pale.

"Take them to the dungeon," he commanded, loud enough so everyone in the great hall could hear. Then he turned back toward me and nodded.

According to our plan, I would go straight to my chamber, escorted by the two guards who flanked my door earlier. I knew I had to listen, but the overwhelming urge to follow behind, to eavesdrop was powerful.

Before I had the chance to follow my instincts to spy, I was greeted by the two guards.

"I'll bring up your meal, my lady," Agatha said. She gathered my plate and cup on a tray and followed behind us.

After what had just happened, I wasn't sure I would be able to eat. Waiting for the hours it would take Logan to interrogate those men was going to be unbearable.

"It would appear ye are the only one I can trust." Logan's voice woke me.

I sat up straighter in the chair, not realizing I'd fallen asleep. He'd come in through the door that connected our rooms, and so I'd not been disturbed by a knock or need to unbar the door.

"Ye didna eat." He motioned toward my dinner plate still full of meat, stewed vegetables and a hunk of bread.

"I wasn't hungry."

"Shall I have Cook send up a warm plate?"

I shook my head. "That's all right."

"No bother, lass. I'm having one sent for myself."

"All right." I stood up, smiling at his thought for me. But now that my head had started to clear, I wanted to know what happened. "Tell me." I stepped closer, placed my hands on his chest and leaned up to kiss his chin.

"The man admitted to threatening ye. His partner was the one he would signal. But he's not the only one. Swore there were more. Some so close to me I'd never imagine."

"Oh no! Who?"

Logan shook his head. "I couldna guess. If they are that close than it would only bring me pain. But a necessary pain." He stroked my cheek sending a thrill of love and temptation skittering over my skin. "I'm serious, though. Ye are the only one I can trust."

"That means a lot to me, Logan." I took a deep breath, trying without success to hold back the words that bubbled on the surface of my tongue. "I can't live without you. I tried. Today, when I left, even though it was forced and I thought to do it to save your life, it killed me inside. You make me happy. I really do love you, so much."

Logan captured my lips in a soulful kiss. "I love ye, too. Together, we can survive anything."

I bit my lip, and leaned in close. "I didn't get a chance to give you your birthday present yet."

"What is it?"

"An appetizer."

"Appetizer?"

"Before dinner treat." I stood back, and smiled seductively as I pulled the laces at the top of my nightgown, revealing the flesh of my breasts.

"Och, the best gift anyone has ever given me." Logan tugged off the rest of my gown and scooped me up in his arms. "And I'm going to savor every last inch of it."

CHAPTER SIXTEEN

Emma

My boots crunched over the gravel walkway in Gealach's small garden. Servants bent over harvesting fall vegetables and herbs that grew in abundance. The scents here were always pleasant, but different with the changing seasons. The sweet, tangy scents of summer were replaced by heartier fall fragrances. Agatha warned me that winter was bound to come soon, and fall was often chilly.

All of what appeared to be September had been beautiful, unusually so. But now into mid-October, the breeze was a tad harsher and the chill sunk in enough that I wore a woolen cloak on especially cool days. Today was one of those days. I stopped to rub my arms, set down the basket of carrots and herbs I'd picked, and glanced around. I'd always taken advantage of the fact that grocery stores were so abundant. Even farmer's markets. I never took the time to actually watch how food was

167

made and provided. There were no stores here, and though there was a market one day a week, most of the food was grown here in the garden or on Gealach lands. No mangoes or avocados, not to mention potatoes and tomatoes, which had yet to make their entrance. The staff was all atwitter when earlier in the summer their lemon trees bore fruit—the trees were a gift from the king. A pleasant treat for these people when I'd come to expect a slice in every glass of water I drank.

The men hunted for meat. When market came, it was most often the crofters selling their wares and food they'd grown that they didn't need or preferred to trade. Men who'd garnered great catches at sea sold fish, eels, oysters and mussels.

It was eye opening, raw, and made me humbler in a way. I appreciated the food on my plate more. The textures, tastes, all so different when they were procured that same day from nature. What I'd heard though was winter was full of stews, salted or dried foods. They worked hard to store enough through spring, summer and fall, so when winter came, they didn't starve.

The kitchen staff had been kind to me, often letting me help in picking, and had even showed me how they baked bread. I'd not yet convinced them to let me help cook anything else or participate much elsewhere, but it did help to keep me occupied, those few chores they'd allow me. The bread I made wasn't half bad. Hearty, thick and filling.

"My lady, his lairdship requests your presence in his library."

Agatha's voice startled me. I'd not heard her approach. I tugged the carrots I'd been uprooting the rest of the way from the ground.

"His library?" Logan had never summoned me there. It was dangerous. The last time I'd even walked near the place I'd almost been gored.

"Aye, my lady. He's expecting ye."

Then hopefully I wouldn't find my guts at my feet. "Will you give this to Cook?" I handed her my basket of goods.

"Of course. I'll see ye in your chamber for the midday meal."

I still took most of my meals alone in my room, with the exception of the feast for Logan's birthday the week before. We'd not seen much of each other since. He spent the majority of his time questioning his men, his clan, and holed up in his library.

I found Ewan waiting outside the library. He nodded and opened the door for me. "His lairdship is expecting ye." The expression on his face was unreadable, and I'd really hoped to have seen a smile. I felt a little like a grade school child about to be punished by the principal.

The room was filled with natural light, the shutters open wide, and a gentle cool breeze washed inside.

"Emma. Come, sit down." Logan pushed back from his chair and came around to give me a slight kiss on the cheek. He pulled out a chair for me and, once he'd seen me settled, walked back around to his desk.

It all felt entirely too formal. Perhaps not a punishment but an expulsion. I swallowed hard, my stomach plummeting and heart squeezing painfully. My mouth was suddenly dry and swallowing felt more like choking.

"You seem so grim." I managed a nervous smile, and gripped the arms of the chair to keep my hands from trembling.

Logan steepled his fingers in front of his face drawing my attention to his bunched biceps beneath a crisply starched white leine. His hair was pulled back tightly in a queue. He studied me with the same vacant expression Ewan wore.

"That bad," I mumbled, suddenly feeling nauseous.

Logan leaned back in his chair, his arms crossing, making me feel even more closed off from him.

"I've had a missive from the king," he said with lips set in a grim line.

Why did it sound so ominous? Was the king requesting my departure?

Logan looked away, something he very rarely did. Damn, it *was* bad.

"What did it say?" I couldn't take his silence. Wished he would just tell me.

"He's planning a visit in the next week."

"Is that all?" A visit seemed hardly that terrible. Even if the king was a tyrant, it wasn't so bad as all that. Why were Logan and Ewan acting so strangely?

"Unfortunately, no, lass. There's more." Again Logan looked away.

I shifted my feet, crossing and uncrossing my ankles. My nerves put me on edge and I was nearly ready to shriek with hysteria and demand he tell me when his gaze met mine once more.

"As ye know, I'm the Guardian of Scotland."

I nodded. What the hell did that have to do with anything? Was he being called away? God, I couldn't live here without him. I wouldn't last.

"Ye see, as the king's man, I must do as he says."

"I understand that." My fingers itched to reach across the table and shake some sense into him. "Don't doubt that I do. Just tell me. The suspense is giving me heart palpitations."

Logan's eyes widened. "'Haps I should tell ye another time. Or call for some wine. I dinna want to overtax ye."

"Just spit it out!" I'd never shouted at Logan in all the time I'd known him. I didn't do it consciously, and I felt utterly terrible for doing it now, but he was literally putting me over the edge.

"He's bringing with him…a woman."

"A woman?" I raised my brows in question. "His lover? His wife?"

"Nay, lass. Ye see, the king wishes for me...to marry."

Marry? An arrow could have struck me. I fell back in my chair as though I'd been shoved, and my insides cramped and knotted painfully. Shock and sorrow were a painful poison.

"You..." I could barely catch my breath. Pressed my hands to my chest to still my beating heart. "You can't be serious."

Logan's voice was low, barely audible. "I am."

After all I'd confessed, all we'd shared. All we'd been through together. We were meant for each other. The magic of the stone circle, me traveling five-hundred years back in time... Our worlds could be torn apart. Forever.

This was worse than me traveling back to the twenty-first century. At least there, I had no chance of being with Logan. I would die if I had to watch him wed another woman, kiss her, make love to her. Know that everything we'd shared, he was now going to share with her...

Needing fresh air, I stood abruptly, my chair wobbling behind me before landing on its four legs. Sanity demanded I leave his presence to catch my bearings. Logan hadn't mentioned that he would fight the king's desires. He hadn't said he would fight for me. Only that the king wished him to marry. Now I knew why he and Ewan had such grim faces. This was the end. Logan would listen to his king. Why would he bother to confess he was in love with me, or even make an inquiry about choosing me as his own. Hadn't he said from the very beginning, the first day we'd met... I could hear his words now. *As a lover, ye are owned by none. I would only ask ye to belong to me and no other. To share your affections with me alone. Until the time we both decide to go our separate ways.*

And now was that time.

The room swayed around me, and bitterness flowed on my tongue. "If you'll excuse me," I murmured, suddenly seeing nothing but blurry blobs. I pushed away from the chair, hurried toward the door and opened it.

"Emma, wait!"

I ignored his calls, dodged Ewan's attempts to pull me back. I could hear Logan running after me, ordering Ewan to stay behind. But I didn't care. I ran.

Logan

"Please open the door." I couldna recall the last time I'd had to beg entrance anywhere, especially into a woman's bed chamber.

But this was wholly different. This, I could understand.

My news had devastated Emma. The way her face had paled, even her rosy lips. It was like watching death roll over her face and my heart had clamped down tight. I'd broken her heart with the words I'd uttered, and yet, there was no way I could pull them back, deny them. They needed to be spoken.

The king would be here in a week's time — or less. And with him, he'd bring a lady who threatened everything important to me. I knew not who she was, and I was sure to dislike her. I'd dislike anyone who was not Emma.

Ballocks, but why the hell did James have to do this to me now? Why did he not give me some warning, ask me to visit his court?

That answer was obvious. It was a rare occasion I went to court due to my needs to be at Gealach, and it was even rarer for James to ask anyone's permission for anything. He was supreme ruler.

Only, he wasn't really.

My coming marriage was yet another way for him to ensnare me. To rule over me. To bend me to his will, and be sure that I was tied even more tightly to his wrists. James would take no chances, that I knew. He'd be sure that I was well and fully tied up. No doubt the bride he had in mind was his own spy. Though she should be virginal, I wouldna put it past the great King of Scotland to have made her his lover first. To trick her into marrying me as a favor. She'd look down on me, think me beneath her, and James would simply sit back and smile.

No sound came from within. I banged again with the side of my fist. "Open the door."

Emma had barred the door leading into the corridor and somehow managed to bar the door between our rooms, but how I couldna imagine.

"Answer me." Sweat beaded on my upper lip. "Please, Emma. Let me know that ye're all right."

"I'm fine." Her voice was distant, but at least I could hear it.

I swiped a hand over my face and leaned my head against the door. "Will ye let me in, so we can talk?"

"There is nothing more to say. You are putting me aside."

"Nay, never."

Silence.

I couldna expect Emma to understand the war within me, between duty to my king and what my heart truly wanted. She'd been guarded when she arrived and I'd worked hard to break her shell, to show her that she should follow her heart, and now here I was contradicting everything I'd ever said.

"I want ye to understand."

"There is nothing to understand." Her voice was closer now.

"Aye, there is. I must honor the king's wishes—" A crash from the other side cut off my words, but I forged on anyway. "I have no other choice. If King James knew of ye..."

How many times had I told Emma that her life was in danger? Would she even believe me now? As if she could hear his thoughts, her bitter words came through the door.

"But it would put me in danger. Is that it, Logan? I'll be unsafe. Someone might try to kill me? Or maybe you? Maybe you're more worried about your own sorry ass than you are about mine. Maybe you were just using me this entire time because it was nice to have a willing body between your sheets. Well, I'm done being your willing body. I told you when I first came here that I refused to be your whore and I wasn't lying. I will not be your hidden secret, your mistress."

"Love, please. Let me explain. James… he is ruthless."

"Aren't all kings and queens?" Her words dripped with sarcasm.

"Aye. But ye see, things are different between James and I." It was time to tell Emma the truth. She had to know what she was up against. "If ye knew the truth, then ye'd understand. Let me explain it to ye." And 'haps, if he was lucky, she'd be willing to stay by his side until they could work things out with James. There had to be some hope…

Though it truly felt hopeless.

A loud scraping came from the other side.

"Emma?"

And then the door opened.

"I'm all ears."

How exactly did one explain that they were the rightful king, traded in for a substitute and then blackmailed into keeping guard of the imposter and his country?

With great difficulty and a jug of whiskey.

CHAPTER SEVENTEEN

Emma

The truth hurt. That was certainly accurate.

Four miserable days had passed since Logan shared with me the secrets behind his birth and place at Gealach. My heart ached for him and what he'd gone through. To lose his parents and the whole life he'd known… And to be stabbed in the back by his own flesh and blood. A twin. Was it possible there could be another man who looked so much like Logan, but was inherently evil on the inside?

I found it hard to fathom.

Thank God they were fraternal twins. There was no doubt in my mind that if they'd been identical, Logan would have been killed long ago. Most babies looked the same. How many had sat on the edges of their seats waiting to see if the two boys looked alike? How many had lain awake at night wondering if the crimes they'd committed against the crown would be discovered?

Logan's poor surrogate mother must have wept with joy when it was realized that the boys were not identical. I couldn't imagine what it must have been like to have been given the gift of a child, a very important child. To have nursed him back to health, laid awake with him when he had a nightmare, wipe away the tears, teach him everything there was to know, and all the while, in the back of your mind wondering if someone was going to come along and snatch him away.

Must have been so hard.

And poor Logan, not having known all along, and then to find out after his "father" had passed, and his mother shortly thereafter. The king, his true father, had died before he was even a toddler. He'd never been able to question them about it. Find out the details. He would most likely never find closure. Not a deal I wished on anyone.

I thought time-travel was the worst shock I'd gotten in my life, but to hear Logan's story... To know that in all my history classes I'd never heard his... It meant that his truth had never been revealed to the world. That he died wondering why he wasn't good enough, and with his brother constantly at his back.

Once more I found myself wishing I'd studied more of Scottish history. More of Gealach's history. If I had, I might have known which path he took. Was his wife's name Emma or some other name? I was just as much in the dark about our future as he was.

And I think we were both equally tortured by it.

I'd bared my soul to him, listened to him bare his soul to me, and I still hadn't told him the whole truth about myself. I'm glad I didn't. This was the ultimate test in both of our fortitudes.

If he chose me and the king allowed it, I would tell him. I couldn't keep it from him then. But if we were separated, I would go quietly back up to the ridge, to the stone circle and pray it took me back to my own time. Fate had to know, if that time came to be, that I no longer belonged here. Destiny wouldn't prolong my pain, would it?

"If ye dinna be careful, you'll make a mush of my herbs," Cook scolded. She stood in front of me, hands on her hips, and a brow raised. I would have been scared of her, if I hadn't known she was such a sweetheart on the inside.

I glanced down to see that I'd rubbed the herbs raw between my fingers, staining my skin green. The scent of sage filled the air around me in a cloud.

"I'm sorry," I murmured, but my apology went unnoticed.

A loud trumpet sounded, dogs barked, children screamed and everyone around me went running. It could only mean one thing. The king had arrived.

"Go, now, my lady. Ye'll not be wanting to greet the king like that!"

I don't know who spoke it, but they were right. I never wore my best gown out in the gardens and I couldn't very well shake the king's hand with stained fingers. No, wait. I couldn't shake his hand. What did one do? Simply curtsey? But hadn't I seen them take the king's hand and kiss his ring?

I felt utterly unprepared. No one had taken the time to prepare me for the king's visit and I was afraid I'd make a fool of myself. Well, I didn't want to meet him anyway. He was bringing another woman for my Logan. Who knew, if he was dead set on the two of them marrying, and he wouldn't listen to Logan's protests, the king might have brought a priest, too.

Yet another painful truth — His Majesty would tear us apart.

I contemplated hiding somewhere in the garden, but a quick glance around showed there wasn't many places to hide that would be comfortable. I could slip behind the row of hedges that lined the wall, but I'd have to stand for hours. I wasn't going to climb one of the nut or fruit trees.

The trumpet sounded again, closer this time than it had been before.

Darn it! I had no other choice but to go inside.

I ran into the castle through the back, dropped my basket in the kitchen and took the servants' stairs up to the level where mine and Logan's rooms were. Guards were still posted there, and when they saw me they stepped aside. Would the king wonder why I had this room? Would he insist the bride he'd chosen for Logan take it? I couldn't bear it. Bile rose in my throat at the thought.

Once inside my room, I ran to the window to look out. A grand procession entered through the gates and milled into the courtyard, surrounded by clansmen, women and children. Liveried horsemen, and some on foot. They held flags on long poles, and in the middle of them all was the most regal man I'd ever seen. He looked straight out of a Renaissance fair. A gold and jeweled crown sat atop glossy, dark hair. Beneath it, a chiseled face that resembled Logan's—only with subtle differences, such as the shape of his nose and the line of his brows. If anyone were to look at that side by side, it had to be obvious they were related. His Majesty's clothes were rich auburn and black velvets with gold embroidery, and his boots reflected the clouds. He had a sword at his side, and an elegant plaid sash was tossed over his shoulder. The king didn't dress like Logan. He looked more like a royal—a king who didn't get his fingers dirty—where Logan looked like a warrior, the epitome of strength.

But what really took my breath, made my knees knock together and had me holding onto the window ledge for balance, was the beautiful woman at his side. She was even more elegant than James. Her dress was blue velvet with white lace and silver trimmings. A plunging neckline, tapered waist and flowing skirt. The sleeves were long and form-fitted, and the shoulders had slashes with different colored fabric coming through. She looked like a queen. I could see from here her breasts, spilled from the top of her gown, providing every man with a very happy view. I just prayed they didn't draw Logan's attention.

I glanced down at the modest gown I wore and realized I undeniably couldn't compare. Not ever. She was the type of woman Logan would marry. I was the type he had sex with. She would marry him, bear his children. I would be the one he came to play with. I could practically see it now. North was the wife and south was the mistress.

I couldn't compete. "I swear I won't."

There was a quick knock at the door. "My lady, 'tis Agatha."

"I'm not feeling well," I called, praying the maid would take my words at face value and go away.

"Now, now, my lady. Ye must open up, else his lairdship will become angry with me for not preparing ye to meet our king."

I rolled my eyes. Agatha played the game well. She knew I'd never want her to suffer for something I did. I begrudgingly unbarred the door and allowed her in. She carried in her arms another new gown in deep navy blue velvet with gold trim and pearls on the bodice. It looked to be very much like the style of dress Logan's bride wore, even similar in coloring.

I'd long since stopped asking where the gowns came from. I didn't want to know who or how many had worn them before me. When it had been offensive at one time, I now understood the value of fabric, ready-made clothes, and the time it took to prepare such things.

Several items I'd received had even been from Logan's deceased mother—well, I guess she wasn't technically his mother, was she? Who was his mother?

Oh. My. God.

I gripped the post of the bed to hold myself upright. If memory served me right... I believed that King James V was the son of Margaret Tudor—daughter of Henry VII of England—sister to Henry VIII!

That meant... Blood drained from my head, making me feel faint. I was in a relationship with someone of the Tudor line. Knowing that, I totally understood how James could treat his brother with such ill-will.

Gealach, Logan, our affair—it all took on a much different light when I thought about it that way.

And... Didn't James V die in 1542? I couldn't remember for sure. And the only reason I recalled it anyway was from visiting Holyrood Abbey in Edinburgh with Steven—where the king was buried along with many others.

But if I was right, all hell was going to break loose soon.

Agatha clucked around, helping me to get ready while I chewed on my lip and bounced between what would happen downstairs in the next hour and what would happen in the next two months. Luckily she took my trembling hands to be fear for meeting the king and not that my entire future hung in the balance.

I hardly saw myself in the mirror when Agatha stood me in front of it. Just a blurred vision of what I was supposed to be. She'd tamed my hair and piled it elegantly atop my head—with pins pinching against my scalp. The gown was cinched giving me the appearance of a full figure and cleavage that I knew was an illusion.

I blinked back the haze and really studied myself. I looked...good. Shockingly. The beauty downstairs wasn't the only one who could wear fancy clothes.

"I might have a chance," I whispered.

"What's that dear?"

"Nothing. Is it time to go?"

"Aye. Ewan has been waiting outside the door."

"I hope not for too long."

But when we opened the door, Logan was also there waiting. He glanced over me with such raw, male appreciation, my body heated and tingled all over.

"Ye look ravishing, Emma."

I bowed my head, hiding my smile and the blush that flamed over my exposed chest.

"Shall we?" He held out his arm and I slid my hand through, loving the feel of strength beneath my fingertips.

And I needed all the strength I could get. Meeting the king was going to be one of the hardest things I'd ever done—the first being running away from my former husband, technically still my husband, if vows transcended time.

This man, this supreme ruler of the country, of all its men, women, children, the maker of laws and the decider if someone lived or died, this man would be looking at me in a few moments' time and judging me. Judging whether or not I was worthy. Judging what he would do with me or to me. He of all people might realize I did not belong.

I swallowed past a lump the size of a grapefruit lodged in my esophagus. "I think I would rather lie down. I'm suddenly not feeling well."

"Nonsense, lass." Logan leaned close, his lips brushing to my ear. His warm breath washed over me in comforting measure. "When we go in, ye can go to the side with Ewan. The king will not look your way, and if he does it will only be with appreciation, for ye are the most beautiful of women. And that dress"—he eyed me hungrily—"is torture to a man's soul."

I tried to smile, to laugh, but all that came out was a choking noise. Pushing me to the side with Ewan was more than just protecting me. He was making sure the king didn't notice me. He'd made his choice. Logan wasn't going to tell the king he'd decided against a marriage of the king's choosing.

181

I felt even more ill to my stomach. If he'd not been holding my arm, I would have run right then and there.

"Look to the ground. Appear meek. He willna bother ye if ye remain modest."

I nodded. He wouldn't notice me at all. And that was most likely Logan's point. He would never show the king, or anyone else for that matter, what I was to him. I thought when he'd brought me in to dinner several days prior that he was showing me things were changing. Our connection in the stone circle, it all pointed to us moving forward. Now we were taking a giant leap backward, and I couldn't help but have hurt pride.

The guards outside the great hall opened the doors for our entry, but before anyone could see us, Logan passed me to Ewan who tucked my arm around his elbow. We followed behind Logan a few steps then moved to the left, remaining in the back of the great hall while Logan walked to the dais to bow to the king and the woman he'd brought with him.

I hated her then. Hated the way she was dressed and her beauty. Hated the jewels that dripped from her ears, glossy dark hair and slender pink neck. Hated the curl of her lips that spoke of sinful anticipation—directed at Logan. Hated that I couldn't see his response. The fact that she continued her perusal with obvious interest meant Logan hadn't made any attempt to dissuade her. And then they were introduced, the king's loud voice booming throughout the room.

"Lady Isabella of Clan MacNeill."

Even her name was elegant. Logan bowed over her hand and brought it to his lips. Lady Isabella visibly shivered. A shiver I knew all too well, for his lips on my hands sent my body into ultra-waves of need.

As if sensing my nerves Ewan tucked me closer. "All will be well."

But his promise was empty.

All was most certainly *not* well.

CHAPTER EIGHTEEN

Emma

Keeping my eyes on the ground, I studied the pretty shoes Agatha had put on me. I'd not noticed before now that they held pretty jewels that sparkled when I wiggled my toes, the movement catching the candlelight. If we'd not been where we were with the unwelcome company in our midst, I might have felt like a princess at a ball. As it was, I was more like Cinderella, except in this fairy tale, she doesn't win.

Ewan stiffened. I looked up sharply at him but saw his gaze was straight ahead. Following his line of vision, I noticed the king was headed straight my way. His gaze was hungry, and conniving. Had he seen the way I reacted when Logan was introduced to Lady Isabella? Was my jealousy so transparent?

"No," I murmured. *Make him turn around!*

Thankfully, he stopped and greeted one of Logan's warriors. I closed my eyes, letting relief flood over me.

Damn it if Ewan didn't stiffen again. I was about to tell him not to stiffen each time the king moved, but he had good cause this time. King James was most definitely making his way toward me, no matter how many people Logan sought to intercede him with.

"I need to go," I whispered frantically to Ewan. I was growing light-headed and pain seared across my forehead.

"Nay, ye must stay. He will only follow."

I tugged at the warrior's arm, but he wouldn't budge. Damn him.

"I don't believe we've met before, my lady." King James had a Scottish accent, but still didn't speak the same as Ewan, Logan, or the rest of the Highlanders. His speech was more refined, more English, despite the slight burr. The way his lips moved made it seem like he was forced to speak that way, rather than it coming naturally to him. His gaze roved hungrily over me, from the top of my head to my toes, lingering too long on my lips, breasts and hips. My stomach turned, and I was very close to puking all over this royal asshole.

"This is Lady Emma." Logan did not expound on my identity.

The king glanced at his brother with interest, obviously taking note of his lack of explanation and then turned back to me with a lecherous smile.

"Lady Emma is a relation of mine," Ewan stepped in quickly. His tone was strong, his hold on my arm tight. "We've not seen each other in quite some time."

I bowed my head and sank down a few inches in some semblance of a curtsey, praying the king took Ewan's meaning of protection to heart. Was there really any hope in it? Didn't kings do as they wished? And King James a nephew of Henry VIII—wouldn't he definitely take what he coveted?

"I see." The king held out his leather-clad hand.

I hesitated to take it. Hoped he would think I was accepting his... What? Offer? He'd not made one, just stared at me like some creepy perv. If I didn't take his hand, he was bound to become angry over it. Ewan nudged me with his elbow as if to answer the questions in my mind.

I took his hand in mine, prepared to kiss the large gold and ruby ring on his finger when he dropped forward and placed a prolonged kiss on my bare wrist. I shivered—and not in a good way. I had to hold my breath, bite down hard on my cheek to keep the bile at bay. I couldn't even look at Logan. Didn't want to see what his reaction would be. Couldn't take the chance that his expression would be indifferent.

After all, this was his brother, wasn't it? Though these two had their issues, would he find fault with the way his brother, his king, was introduced to me?

I desperately hoped so, but still couldn't take the chance he wouldn't.

The king did not let go of my hand, but instead tugged me a little closer, and then whispered in my ear.

"You are a beautiful, ripe woman. I'd like to pluck you right from your cousin's arm. I expect you won't deny your king an audience. Come to my room in the next hours' time. I find I'm in need of a woman's charms."

My stomach rolled. I couldn't move. Not even to nod my head in false affirmation.

A movement caught my eye and I looked up to see that Logan had taken a step forward. "Your Grace, if ye dinna mind, I'd like to take ye to my library. There is much to discuss."

I could have kissed him for his attempt to intervene, but I would have only been pushed aside by the king's cruel smile as he glanced between the two of us.

"Is Lady Emma your mistress?" He was sly as a snake, and took obvious pleasure in our discomfort.

Lady Isabella who'd been milling in the background shoved beside Logan at hearing that. Logan's eyes were filled with piercing anger. I'd seen it before when someone crossed him. He didn't like the situation any more than I did, but yet, he said nothing. To say something would have—

"We've not yet been introduced," Lady Isabella said smoothly. Her voice dripped with sticky sweetness, yet her eyes betrayed her. She was one-hundred percent bitch. "I'm Laird Gealach's betrothed." The bitch looked all around her as if to say that one day this castle would be hers.

What was the saying? If you make your bed, prepare to lie in it? If Logan was refusing to fight for me, maybe he deserved her.

"Papers have yet to be signed," Logan interjected, his voice was cool, calm, belying the rage I saw burning in his eyes.

Lady Isabella and the king both ignored Logan.

"'Tis a certainty," Lady Isabella said with such authority I would have taken a step away if Ewan hadn't held tight to my arm.

I wasn't a violent person, but I wanted so very much at that moment to punch her right in the mouth. Logan seethed beside her, speechless—or at least holding back whatever it was he wanted to say. The king watched our interaction with undisguised interest and Ewan squeezed me closer, as if knowing I would indeed relish hitting this beautiful monster.

"Lovely to meet you. I was simply passing through." I tried to make my voice sound less American. Hoped it sounded more like them. I paused a moment, waiting for someone to yell imposter, but no one did. "I'm afraid, we won't be able to spend much time together as I'll be leaving the castle soon."

"Pity." Isabella's lips curled in a cruel and triumphant smile.

"Indeed." I don't know where I got the strength to play Isabella's games, because in truth, I wanted to fall to my knees and slip between the cracks in the floorboards, disappearing into the bowels of the castle forever.

Logan

Fury made my vision red and hollowed the noise from within the great hall to sound more like ominous echoes rather than voices. How dare James and Isabella barge into Gealach and make such unfounded statements?

I'd had my hands clenched for the better part of the hour, just to keep from drawing my sword. I was close to tossing the high-handed woman out on her rear. Lady Isabella of Clan MacNeill was one of the last women I would ever marry— MacDonald's daughters taking the first slots in that category. Clan MacNeill was one of MacDonald's staunch supporters. Which made them my enemies.

And now, Emma had stated that she was leaving. Her eyes were empty, mouth flat and thin, uncaring, indifferent. When she'd opened her door and come out in the gorgeous gown I had made just for her, her skin had color, eyes lighted on me, and there was joy in her. Now all sign of happiness had left her.

'Twas obvious that in her mind she'd already gone. Been set aside. But she wasn't. Not in the least. I couldn't have her thinking such nonsense. And yet, if I said anything to contradict Emma, my brother would know how special she was, and take her as some sort of punishment for me not readily agreeing to the marriage with Isabella.

"Your Grace, if I may have a word with ye?" I had to get James alone. Had to make him see reason. Marrying into the MacNeill clan—aligning myself with our enemy—was not in the best interest of Scotland nor Gealach.

"Not, now," James muttered with a wave of his hand. "A toast!"

I was so easily dismissed by him. The bastard. Inside I seethed, my guts eating away at themselves. Servants rushed to bring him a goblet and wine. While I tried hard not to glare at them all for allowing *King* James to take over. I was never more powerless than when James was in the room. I glanced down at his waist where his broadsword with the ornately designed gold handle rested. A swipe of my hand and I'd have his own sword at his throat. Demand my kingdom returned to me.

As James raised his glass, and I refused to take one, shouts rang out from the courtyard. An icy chill slid down my back. The king glanced at me, fear in his eyes. For all his bluster, he was nothing more than a coward bending people to his will with threats. The gate would already be closed with the king visiting, which meant the possibility our enemy was attempting to lay siege.

Angus rushed into the great hall, out of breath, and face blustery. "My laird! They've come."

"To arms!" I bellowed and my men, shaking off the haze of mystique James and Isabella deluded them with, ran for the doors.

"Take her to her room," I ordered Ewan. I didn't dare look at Emma, nor speak to her, for fear the king would take notice and offer to watch over her—which only meant he'd try to seduce her and when that didn't work, take her by force.

"Aye, my laird." Ewan whisked Emma up the stairs, followed by the two guards who constantly lurked behind her now.

I watched my brother's gaze follow her for a moment before he snapped and two of his own guards stepped forward. "Take Lady Isabella to her chamber and guard her there." He glanced at me. "You had a room prepared for your future wife, did you not?"

I nodded, and summoned the attention of one of the maids. "Take Lady Isabella to her chamber."

The room prepared for her was well away from mine. Thank the Gods.

The king's men followed Isabella from the great hall with the maid chasing after. Isabella acted as though she'd already settled in and knew exactly where she was to be housed. No matter, I had a castle and clan to defend, and no time for conniving females.

As I passed through the entry hall to the castle main doors, I smirked. Lady Isabella had in fact finally seized the maid to point her in the right direction. The woman wouldna be here long, and never on a permanent basis.

But the smirk fell from my face as I stepped onto the ledge, flaming arrows were falling like shooting stars from the sky. There was only one man who could be attacking now — Allan o' the Wisp. He'd escaped us thus far, my ship never being found. Well, 'twould appear he'd yet decided to bless us with his presence.

"Bastard." I made haste to shout orders. "To the well! Get buckets of water and put out the flames. Men, shields! If ye're not a warrior, get inside the castle."

Several people writhed on the ground, pinned to the soggy earth with flaming arrows that melted the clothes on their backs and painfully licked away their flesh. I whipped off my plaid, my shirt covering me to the knees, but I could have really cared less who saw my bare arse. I patted my plaid down on one burning body after another, but, to most, the damage was already done and they were gone, or so badly burned, they begged for the mercy of my sword to rescue them.

How had we been undermined once more by our enemy? Security should have been even higher with James' presence.

Chaos was all around as men shot arrows from atop the battlements and then sought to shield themselves from the flaming sprays of our enemy. Ladders must have been pushed up to the walls as my men shoved at bodies climbing over.

I started for the gate tower, where it appeared more men were climbing than my guards could handle, but a hand gripped forcefully at my elbow held me back.

"Brother," I seethed. "Let me go. We need not lose any more of our people."

James shook his head.

"Dinna ye see?" I held my free arm out, exasperated. "This is MacDonald's work. He's a danger, and ye'd have me marry the daughter of his ally — our enemy."

James bristled, his grip still tight to my arm. "Ye must protect the king." He said nothing of his order to marry their enemy.

"That is what I intend to do." I pulled free and started to walk toward the gate, when again, he pulled me back.

"You will protect me here."

"Are ye mad? They will overtake the wall by the gate tower if I dinna help." Was it possible James wanted this? That he'd turned against me entirely?

James seemed to search for something to say, his eyes, darting back and forth. So much was hidden in their depths, in his mind.

A blood curdling scream sounded from behind, and I turned in time to see that my men had been overtaken by the gate tower — tossed to their deaths outside of the walls.

"Go inside, my king. I will protect ye, but I canna do it here."

James seemed to come to his senses, nodding. I didna wait for him to go inside, but ran toward the gate tower. They couldna be allowed to open the gates. There was no telling how many stood on the other side. We'd be accepting certain death if we did. I fought my way up the stairs, parrying left and right with my sword, striking hard with my dirk, and crushing noses with my fists. I, too, tossed men over the rails into the courtyard below, and over the walls into the moat. Soaked in blood, I reached the battlements and fought my way through four men before reaching the ladder and hacking at those who climbed until it was unbalanced enough for me to push it back.

None had been able to get over. Those in the moors beyond prepared arrows.

"Archers!" I bellowed, calling to my own for retaliation. They prepared their bows; notching arrows and drawing back their strings, they let their own flaming missiles fly.

"Shields!" I called when our enemy released their flames, and all who stood, held up their various steel and wood shields to protect themselves. Even still a few screams were heard as arrow tips dug into flesh and muscle.

"Archers!" The orders happened again and again. Ladders continued to push up to the stones, and we continued to push them back.

Allan made himself known, riding into the center of the field, his hair flying wild. He saw me and made an obscene gesture.

"Are ye suffering yet, Grant?" he bellowed from the field.

I should have killed him when I had the chance. "Nay. Ye failed, Allan!"

The man snarled and ordered his men to shoot another round.

I seized a bow and arrow from the archer who'd stood beside me and took aim. How I wanted to take him down for the evil dog he was. I let out a slow breath, then let go. The arrow flew from the bow, its feathers swishing by my cheek as it went. Allan saw it coming, made an attempt to move, but it was too late. My arrow struck him in the center of his chest, the force shoving him from his horse. He fell backward over the mount, landing on the ground in a stream of blood.

What seemed like hours later, the last of our enemy ran away. Defeated.

I shook with fatigue, my breathing labored, vision red from the blood that ran into my eyes. My hands were unrecognizable.

"Gather the dead." My voice was labored, throat raw.

But we were all still alive.

And I had a king's mind to alter.

CHAPTER NINETEEN

Emma

A soft knock startled me away from the window where I watched the chaos and violence raging on below. Without thinking, I unbarred the door to see Lady Isabella in the hallway. Up close I could see her eyes were a dull grey, lifeless. I almost felt bad for her. What must her life be like to be nothing more than a pawn? Any sympathy I had for her disappeared though when she smiled like a cat who'd eaten the canary. Opening the door had been a mistake.

"What do you want?" I asked, not bothering to hide my frown. We weren't in front of the king or a room full of people. There was no more need for polite show.

My guards stood still as statues, pretending not to be there.

"May I come in?" Her voice was ultra-calm and smooth. It was enough to make me cringe.

"No." I wasted no time in answering her. There wasn't anything to think about. I made a move to close the door, but she pushed in anyway, forcing me to take a step backward.

The bitch shut the door quietly, then turned to face me, her hands folded at her waist looking entirely too peaceful for whatever reason had her standing in my bedroom.

"I see your room is close to the laird's."

"How—" She cut me off with a lift of her hand and took a menacing step forward.

Sinking into my old habits, I took a step back, prepared to give in. But the new me fought to the surface and I returned to my position and stared her dead in the eyes.

"I make it my business to know everything about everyone. Don't try to deny that your room is beside the laird's. Don't try to deny that you're his lover. Simply know that you will never see him again. And if you so much as try to contact him, I will personally see that you are whipped for the whore that you are." Isabella's voice was quiet as she hissed her words.

My heart leapt into my throat. Isabella was so confident that she and Logan would be married. Had, in fact, stated it for a certainty in front of the king. It was a settled matter in their eyes, and since Logan hadn't bothered to deny it, in his as well. I didn't doubt that this heinous wench would try her damndest to make good on her threats.

I decided to go with self-preservation, and right now my pride needed the boost. Time to have fun with this hoity-toity snot.

"Oh, my dear, you have nothing to worry about, concerning me. Logan on the other hand..." I let my voice trail off and offered her a look of condolence.

Isabella looked taken aback for a moment, but only a split-second before she slid back into her cool demeanor. She was good at hiding her emotions, once more her vulnerability hidden behind a face fueled by bitterness.

"I'm not entirely certain I understand your meaning." Isabella sounded so proper I wanted to puke.

But I had to stand strong to continue on with my taunts — readily admitting to myself they were driven by jealousy.

"You see, I really was leaving. I prefer a lover with…different tastes."

Isabella's brows drew together. "To what are you referring?"

Somehow I knew. I don't know how, call it woman's intuition, but this lady knew a heck of a lot more about being with a man than any virginal noble woman should.

I stepped forward, hinting at sharing something intimate. "He prefers the company of… Oh, dear, I just can't say it." I bit my lip and sucked in a breath. I pressed my hands over top each other onto my belly. "It's truly vile."

"Vile?" I was surprised by the hungry spark in her eyes. Lady Isabella was not only *not* a virgin, she liked vile…

Damn… How could I make this work?

"Pigs." I blurted it out and then clapped my hands over my mouth. "He likes pigs."

The woman took a jolted step back, her face screwed up with disgust. What luck, that had come from nowhere…

"You came in just the nick of time. I was preparing a way to tell him I could no longer remain, and then, poof" — I snapped my fingers – "here you are to save me."

Isabella put her hands on her hips and gave me a disbelieving look. Had I taken it too far? Now she didn't believe me?

"I've never heard of it. Why wouldn't anyone ever talk about this?"

I shook my head vehemently. "Oh, no. They wouldn't. He's threatened to kill me and all of my family if I ever did."

"Ah-ha! You lie." She pointed at me. "You wouldn't risk your own neck to tell me."

I nodded. "Normally, you would be right." I reached out and grasped her hand, pretending at being a lady seeking another's confidence. "But no one has ever married him. Lovers come and go. Marriage is forever."

Isabella blanched. She blinked a few times, then licked her lips. "Well, I see. I really must be going. Thank you for warning me."

I inclined my head, a peaceful nod and a sweet smile that would have irritated me, had I seen it on her, and murmured, "You're welcome."

Damn, but it felt good to best Isabella. She was such a nasty piece of work, and without even knowing me, she was bent on hurting me.

But that didn't matter. I still had to leave. Even if my little ruse felt good, it didn't mean that Isabella would go against the king's orders, or that the king would give permission for their betrothal to be broken. If anything, I could smile with some bit of triumph at the fear she'd feel every time Logan came to her chamber. *Ugh.* I felt sick all over again. Imagining him with another woman was just too painful.

Despite what Fate had showed me in the stone circle, it would appear that I didn't have a place here. I was not going to be Logan's mistress if he was married to another. No matter how much I loved him. It was a matter of principle. I didn't want to share him. If I couldn't have him to myself, then I just couldn't have him, no matter how much it crushed my soul to think it.

I whipped open the wardrobe and sifted frantically through every gown, chemise and cloak. There had to be a bag in here. Something I could take with me if time travel wasn't possible. I had to be realistic. I'd tried so many times now, and I was still here. Taking the clothes and cloak would, technically, be stealing, but I couldn't very well go off into this sixteenth century world without some possessions. I supposed, bitterly, I could consider it payment for services rendered.

No bag. *Darn it!*

I faced the room, hands on my hips and blew a stray hair out of my face. This was pointless. It wasn't like I could get out now. There was a battle going on.

Oh, crap. Logan! I was supposed to be distancing myself from him, but not in this. I couldn't sit back when his life was on the line and pretend nothing was happening. I ran back to the window in time to see him toss the last of the enemy from the battlements and then begin issuing orders, arm up in the air and then pointing forward. Flaming arrows flew over the walls in retaliation and Logan and his men held up their shields, ducking at the last minute as the sound of the bolts landing echoed. I couldn't watch. Only pray.

Slamming the shutters closed I turned around, hands flat to the stone wall and closed my eyes. But standing there waiting only stressed me out even more. I needed to do something, anything, to distract myself.

I picked up all the clothes I'd thrown out of the wardrobe and reorganized them. Straightened my bed again. Stacked the wood in the hearth. Washed my hands and face. Braided my hair. A million little things to keep me busy, with the sounds of pain and plunking of arrows always a distant buzz. When the shouting from outside ceased and all appeared calm. I simply waited. Logan would come to my room. He had to. Just like he did all the other times.

And I would tell him that I had to leave. This time I wouldn't let him win. I'd remind him of our agreement, no matter how much it hurt to take our love out of the equation. I wasn't going to stay. I'd remind him he was to be married and things between us would have to be different. But I did want him for myself one *last* time.

Agatha came and brought me dinner. Her eyes were tired and her mouth in a grim line. She knew I was leaving, I could sense it, so I didn't say anything, but thanked her kindly for all she'd done for me.

After picking at the cold venison stew and sipping wine for an hour, the door between our rooms slowly opened and Logan filled the entryway. His broad shoulders took up the expanse of the frame. A look of concern crinkled his eyes in the corners. His hair was wet, and the alluring scent of his soap made me take a deep breath in. He'd not bothered to put on a shirt, but wore a plaid, loosely belted at his hips. His feet were bare. Ultra casual, as though he couldn't wait to finish dressing until he spoke with me.

One last night. That was all. A parting gift to myself.

"I'm glad you're safe." I stood up from the chair and smoothed my skirt. My stomach did a little flip.

Logan stepped into the room making it suddenly feel smaller. "We need to talk."

I shook my head and when I spoke, my voice sounded small. "There is nothing to say."

"Ye're wrong. There is much."

But I didn't want to talk. Not now. I closed the space between us, touched my hand to his chest. I didn't want to have this conversation. I just wanted to savor one last night in his arms. Tomorrow, I'd figure out how to get out of here unnoticed.

"Kiss me."

Logan frowned. He took my hands in his. "Emma, please, let me speak."

I shook my head, leaned up on tiptoe and pressed my lips to his. For the first time, Logan attempted to resist. A clue that he truly wanted to talk. But I didn't want to listen. He was only going to tell me that he had to do what his brother wanted, that there was no other way, and he was going to try to convince me to stay.

And I wouldn't.

I slipped my tongue over his lips, pressed my hips up into his, cradling his hard cock with my pelvis. He might have tried to resist me, but his body wouldn't let him. I moaned against his mouth, slid my hand down the front of his chest to grip his thick shaft. I knew what would make him forget.

Logan gave in, thrusting his tongue into my mouth, swirling and tasting, as he shoved his hands into my hair, untangling the braid I'd done.

"Emma," he breathed. "Oh, my precious, love."

I stroked up his back, massaging the muscles along his spine, feeling them ripple as he did the same to me. I would always remember him this way, the sinew, the warmth, the solidness that I loved.

If this was going to be our last time, I was going to take the lead. I gripped his belt, whipped it open, and let it drop to the floor. His plaid unfurled, falling with a soft breeze around my ankles.

I smoothed my hands down his back, over his taut buttocks and squeezed. Logan growled, and I moaned in turn. My need to take control was powerful. I pulled from his embrace and pushed him toward the bed.

"Lay down," I said, my voice husky. "I'm going to have my way with you."

Logan smiled and winked. "A temptation I am most willing to give in to."

I grinned, though a touch of sadness threatened to take hold. "Good. Now get on that bed."

I pushed him backward, my hands on his chest, following his retreating steps until his knees hit the mattress. He sank back, his hands behind his head and grinned up at me with eager excitement. His cock stood tall and proud, jutting from his middle like a sword, ready to conquer my body.

"Ye've got on too many clothes."

"Don't worry about that." I took a step back and slowly removed my garments, watching his eyes darken with need.

When I was completely nude, I slid my way on top of him, spreading my thighs so I straddled his hips. His cock pressed to my wet sex, begging entry. But I wasn't ready yet. I pressed my breasts to his chest, letting the crisp hairs tickle my hardened nipples. When I pressed my lips to his neck, his pulse pounded, I lingered there, loving the feel of how I affected him. I nipped at his earlobe and then kissed his mouth hard.

It was such a change to be the one in control. I was shocked that he was allowing it. Excited at the same time.

"You can touch me," I murmured against his lips.

"Where?" He untucked his hands from behind his head.

"Anywhere." I sighed.

Logan gripped my buttocks gently, stroking over my hips and thighs, scraping me with the backs of his nails and sending shivers and goosebumps all over me. Up my ribs to my breasts he went, tickling, massaging.

I pushed forward, putting my breasts near his mouth, and he did as I silently requested, flicking his tongue over my nipple and sucking gently, then harder.

I moaned, arching my back, and rubbing my pelvis against his. What sweet sin it was. Back and forth, I slid, tempting us both. Logan lifted his hips in time with my rocking. Our breathing grew labored and, at last, I reached between us, gripped his cock and guided it to my opening. Logan stilled. I'd expected him to surge upward, but he waited.

"Lass," he said through gritted teeth. "Let me come inside ye."

"Yes," I said, smoothing his lips with mine. "Yes."

Logan gripped my hips and pushed upward at the same time I sank down. Pleasure radiated through me, making my thighs tremble. My fingers sank into his chest and I ground my pelvis against his. Every time we made love, I was shocked and awed by how magical it was. How complete and bursting of pleasure and giving. Both of us sought to see the other one happy and fulfilled. Overcome with wonder, I gazed into Logan's eyes, saw the love I felt radiating there, and it was almost too much to bear.

I closed my eyes and leaned my head back, giving in to pleasure and forgetting the rest, but knowing I'd forever carry with me what it was like to truly be in love.

I arched my back, undulated my hips. We matched rhythms, him pumping up, me back and forth. Naturally, our pace quickened, as we both sought to ease the frantic pressure building in our loins. Logan leaned up on one elbow, skated his hand through my hair with his free hand and tugged me toward him for a deep, soul-quenching kiss.

With the touch and stroke of our tongues, my body responded with an electric shock, coiling and unfurling ecstasy within me. I rode it out, faster, harder, and Logan, too, thrust deep and quick, until he groaned against my lips.

I squeezed my eyes tight, willing the tears building to cease, not wanting him to see that I was so greatly affected, and then wonder at the cause.

"I love you," I murmured, "so much."

"I will never love another, Emma."

CHAPTER TWENTY

Logan

"I'm going to tell the king."

Emma lay beside me, our sweat-slick limbs entangled on top of her coverlet.

"What?" Her voice came out raspy and filled with disbelief. She tried to push up, but I tugged her back into the crook of my arm.

"I have to. I canna marry Lady Isabella."

Emma shook her head, her soft hair stroking back and forth over my shoulder and a waft of her lemon scented soap filled my nostrils.

"Why would ye deny it?" I frowned. "Do ye no longer want me?"

"That's not it," she rushed. "I don't want you to be at odds with the king. Despite your history, he is believed to be the king, and I'm...afraid of his reaction."

"But he must understand that the woman he has chosen for me is wrong on several levels. For one thing, she is not ye. For another, her family is allied to MacDonald. If I were to marry her, I'd be marrying the enemy and inviting them all within the walls of Gealach."

Emma hissed a breath. "I didn't realize..."

"I don't understand the king's determination for me to marry her." I lazily stroked her back as I recalled James trying to stop me in the courtyard. "He is not himself."

"Stress can change a person."

"Aye, but would it make a person choose to betray their entire country, their blood?" James' desperate eyes haunted me.

"I don't know about that. Sounds like something deeper you might be missing."

I nodded, staring up at the ceiling. "I will speak with him. Tell him that I canna possibly marry her. That in order to carry out my duties to Scotland the marriage is not possible."

"I..." Emma hesitated, and my stomach tightened in anticipation of what she could say. "Lady Isabella paid me a visit."

"When?" I stiffened. The viper visiting Emma was bound to be bad.

"During the battle. She made threats. But I made it clear to her I had no designs on you. I may have said something that would make you angry."

"What?" I practically choked out the word, expecting to hear Emma say she was behind the entire ring of spies.

There was a long silence before she answered. "I told her you were not a good lover. That you preferred the company of pigs."

A burst of laughter escaped me and a sharp rush of relief. I tugged her close and buried my face in her hair. A rush of love made me feel elated. "That was nay what I expected to hear at all."

"So you aren't mad?"

I pressed a kiss to her forehead, a smile curling my lips. "Nay. Never. 'Tis something I shall laugh about for years to come."

Emma slid her hand around my waist and squeezed. "Thank goodness. I thought for sure you would fly through the roof when you found out."

"I only wish I could have seen her face when ye told her."

Emma giggled and then tugged the covers up over us, cocooning us in warmth. "She looked stunned, sickened. I'm so sorry."

"Dinna be, I am glad to hear ye shocked her. She's incredibly arrogant. We've yet to sign a treaty and already she is calling herself mistress."

"I do believe your brother set her up to it. He was pretty positive of the fact, too."

"Aye… But, Emma." I rolled to my side, facing her. "I will tell the king I'm not marrying Isabella of MacNeill, and that instead, I will have ye as my wife."

Emma jolted backward. "No. You must not tell him that." This time when she pushed up on her elbow I let her. Her crystal blue eyes blazed with seriousness and concern. "Don't get me wrong, I would love nothing more than to be with you forever. If we lived in a different time, if the king was different, if *we* were different, I would run away with you, beg you to forget all of this and live a simple life in a hovel filled with love, honesty, and without enemies. But that isn't reality."

"Emma—"

"No, let me finish. King James asked me to…visit him. If you tell him you want to marry me, he will only find a way to punish you for it. If all you've told me is true, that is what he'll do. He reminds me so much of — "

She didn't say it, but I knew she must have meant her husband. The evil man who hurt her so much before he died. Though I knew James must have asked her to lie with him, I had a hard time letting that truth sink in. James made it clear in his actions in the great hall that he had a clue Emma was important to me. He asked her to his bed to spite me.

"Emma, I know ye're scared. But I'm willing to give up everything for ye. To face my brother's wrath. I hold his secrets, I can destroy him if I choose."

"Then why haven't you?"

"Because he is my brother. And because if I destroy him, he will destroy me."

"And now you're willing to do that?" She shook her head. "I won't be the cause of your country's destruction. Your destruction. Don't say anything about us. Tell him you can't marry her because of MacDonald, but please, for both our sakes, don't tell him about us."

Emma's hands, pressed so delicately to my chest, shook, and her eyes held a plea for me to give in.

"All right." The words were out of my mouth before I could pull them back. "But if that is what ye want, at least let me share with ye more about the secret of Gealach." I'd already told her half of it, now she might as well know the rest of what I knew.

She shook her head. "No. You said if you ever told me, it could mean both of our deaths."

"But it seems, death may well be coming for me. Like it or not, love, our enemies are so very near."

Emma

Both of us dressed and night having descended on all of Gealach, we crept from my chamber, with only the light of the moon to guide us. The guards who stood outside the doors nodded to their laird, and then went back to staring at the walls when Logan gave them a signal. He didn't mean for them to follow us as he usually did.

Gealach looked completely different in moon shadow. Eerie, ominous. A draft whirled around our ankles, and silence fell hushed over the castle as though it were abandoned.

"Ye've taken note of the designs on the bed post, aye?" Logan whispered.

"Yes," I whispered back.

"They are a map to the doors. A story of what lies behind each of the four. One post for each door."

I had noticed they were similar symbols, and wondered at their meaning. We descended the stairs, a scary feat in the pitch black. I felt at any moment I would slip and push into Logan's back knocking him off balance and we'd both fall to our deaths. But I never slipped, and at last we reached the great hall.

Before entering, Logan pulled me into a hidey-hole where he looked through a slit in the wall. "All is clear," he murmured.

"Can I see?" Those sort of medieval facets always fascinated me.

Logan grinned. "Aye."

We switched places, and I put my eye up to the hole, gazing in on the great hall, dimly lit by a banked hearth. All appeared quiet.

Taking me by the hand, Logan led me silently into the great hall. We slid along the walls, staying close to the shadows and making sure not to disturb any of the servants who slept on the far side, huddled under blankets in front of the fire. Once behind the infamous tapestry, Logan must have found the secret stone and pressed it in, because he pulled me through the opening, and then a massive whoosh of air blew past my cheeks as he closed the door again.

"Stay still," he said.

Seconds later the stairwell lit. He held a torch.

"Where did you get that?" I asked, disappointed I'd not seen it before on my own trek down here.

Logan pointed up above the door where several torches were stashed in a cutout in the stone. I'd never seen it before and the torches were so high up, I probably wouldn't have been able to reach them anyway.

"Let us go." He held my hand and led me down the one-hundred stairs until we reached the small circular room with the four doors.

"Do you have the key?"

He glanced back at me with a grin. "Aye." He pulled a dirk from his boot.

"Are you going to pick the lock?" I asked with a laugh.

"Magic." He twisted the handle and it popped off, revealing a key soldered to the end of the blade. But before I could study it further, he twisted the handle back in place.

Logan went straight for the first door on the left. "This door leads to nothing. A pit, twenty feet beneath us. If 'tis opened, the person drops to their death. See the triquetra?"

He pointed to a design of Celtic swirls in the shape of a triangle.

"Does it mean death?"

Logan grinned, the golden light of the torch glowing in his eyes. "'Tis a trick, for it also means life."

My throat felt tight and I was grateful to never have gotten the courage to break the lock and open the doors.

Logan passed over the second door and the third, but stopped at the fourth. The last symbol on it was a rune — shaped almost like a moon, and identical to the one on my hip.

"I knew from the moment I saw the mark on your hip that ye were meant for me. Behind this door is the treasure. A box with a key that I dinna have."

"Who has it?"

"The king." He traced his fingers over the symbols. "If he were to die, I have instructions to open the treasure and destroy it."

"Destroy a treasure?"

He nodded. "I think 'tis not a true treasure, but some matter of proof that could destroy him. But he's kept me in the dark. Not allowed me to know the whole of it."

Now was the time to tell him the darkest of my secrets, for I, too, had kept him in the dark. "Logan, I need to tell you something. I've tried so many times before now."

He waited patiently. Not like every other time, when he'd tried to hush me with his kiss.

"I told you I'm not from here. But what I should have said was I'm not from your time."

His face did not change, nor show any emotion. He studied me, waiting for me to finish. I took a deep breath and let it all out.

"I am a time traveler. I traveled through time."

Still he didn't budge. I could have been speaking to a statue. I needed some sort of reaction. It'd taken me this long to tell him.

"Emma..." He trailed off, broke eye contact.

Oh, God... He didn't believe me! "Logan, please — "

He shook his head, held up his hand. "How?"

"I don't know. I was running through a storm toward your castle — but it was different, it was the castle in my time, and — "

"And ye woke up here?"

I nodded. "Yes."

"And ye expect me to believe ye?" Still no change to his expression.

I sucked in a breath. "Yes. I do." God, he must think me insane.

"'Tis a hard thing to ask a man."

"I know. But you witnessed magic at the stone circles. Think about it, I'm not a liar. Look at me."

He regarded me with his serious eyes for so long, I was afraid we'd both turn to dust. "That would explain a lot."

I blanched. "That's it? You believe me?"

"Did ye want more, love?"

"Yes," I said, slightly exasperated. "I expected you to deny it, to tell me I'm insane, to try to kill me."

Logan's lip curled in a half smile. "I've always thought ye were a little different. That ye were special. That ye came here for me. I didna know how. Or why. But when I saw ye in that circle, when I realized that ye were begging to go home, and when ye remained, I knew Fate intervened." He paused a moment, his gaze studying me with fondness. "Ye've changed. I've changed. And both of us are the better for it."

I took a step back, disbelieving how calm he was. "It doesn't bother you?"

He shrugged. "Should it?"

"What if I am suddenly gone?"

Logan looked a little stricken, as though he'd not thought of that possibility. "Do ye want to be?"

"No," I choked out. "I don't."

"Fate had ye remain when ye begged to go. I canna see her taking ye from me when we both wish ye to stay."

"But destiny is not always in our favor."

Logan set the torch inside a sconce I'd not noticed before and then took a step closer to me, enfolding me in his arms.

"Ye're right about that. What year did ye come here from?"

"2013."

Logan let out a low whistle. "I'm a bit old for ye, then, aren't I?"

I laughed and kissed him on the chin. "Never too old."

"If such should happen that ye are no longer with me, then I will mourn your loss a moment. But I will also never stop trying to find a way to get ye back or come find ye in 2013."

"Oh, Logan." I hugged him tight, listening to the pound of his heartbeat. "I pray it never comes to that."

"Me too, lass, me too." He kissed me urgently, hotly, lovingly and I threw myself wholeheartedly into it.

He slid his lips from my mouth to my ear and declared, "I'll never let anyone take ye from me. I'll send them to Hell before I ever let that happen. No one will ever tear us apart."

"We'll win together," I said, pressing my hands to his stubbled cheeks.

"We must be strategic. We must stay strong." He pressed his forehead to mine. "Our road will not be an easy one. There are many against me and will be many who oppose us being together. Even those on our side might not see the merit in me turning away an alliance."

"Why?"

"They may think an alliance will bring peace to our clan. That the fighting with MacDonald will stop. But it won't. He will never cease until I'm dead, and I'll continue to fight him until he's buried."

"Stubborn," I teased, trying to make light of the crazy situation.

Logan winked and grinned wickedly. "I prefer determined."

"That you are." I threaded my hand into his hair, entangling his locks around my fingers.

"I'm determined to be with ye."

I bit my lip, emotion welling in my chest. Though, it seemed to be assumed, we'd never really defined what being with each other meant, other than our conversation months before where I accepted being his lover. "As more than a lover?"

"Aye." His voice was low, quiet, serious.

We were really going to do this. It seemed too good to be true, and someone once told me, if it seemed that way, it probably was. There were so many obstacles standing in our way. A major one in particular. "But King James…"

Logan kissed me tenderly, and I sank against him, letting him nibble at my lips. "I'll deal with my brother in time."

I didn't dare ask how much time. I was too afraid of putting a limit on it. I definitely wasn't ready for the repercussions confronting the king was going to bring. And yet, I didn't want to wait forever. I was a walking, breathing bag full of contradictions. "And the treasure?"

"I swear we'll discover its secret together."

A giddy twitter seized my belly. "I feel like we're embarking on an adventure."

Logan's grin widened. "Och, lass, we've already begun."

While this may be *The End* for now — 'tis not truly over…
Look for the final installment of Logan and Emma's story:
The Dark Side of the Laird (December, 2013)

If you enjoyed **BARED TO THE LAIRD**, *please spread the word by leaving a review on the site where you purchased your copy, or a reader site such as Goodreads or Shelfari! I love to hear from readers too, so drop me a line at* authorelizaknight@gmail.com *OR visit me on Facebook:* https://www.facebook.com/elizaknightauthor. *I'm also on Twitter:* @ElizaKnight. *Sign up for my newsletter at*

<u>www.elizaknight.com</u> do get updates on new releases and contests. *Many thanks!*

Book Three: *Dark Side of the Laird*

Bound by passion. Freed by love.

When the damaged and tormented Emma first meets the equally broken Logan, they embark on a torrid, emotionally provocative affair that irrevocably changed their lives. Emma has sacrificed her entire being and just when she thinks Logan is willing to do the same, he holds back. Reluctant for their love to be a thing of shadows, Emma issues an ultimatum: commit or say goodbye. Fearful of losing her, Logan agrees.

In order to keep her, he must gain permission to marry from the one man he's sought to avoid: his brother, the King. His appeal is denied and instead, Logan is seized and sent to the dungeon with no hope for escape. While in Hell, Logan's dark past haunts him, threatening to consume him. He must fight to remain the man he's become with Emma by his side and relinquish the control he's held onto for a lifetime.

Fearing her lover is dead, Emma decides once and for all she must leave history where it belongs and return to the present. But when she tries once again to break the bonds of time, she is struck down. Emma must choose her destiny. Must answer the cries her body makes in the dark for her laird. They've always been strongest when together, but now Emma must find the courage on her own to see her fate fulfilled—and Logan returned to her.

ABOUT THE AUTHOR

Eliza Knight is the multi-published, award-winning, Amazon best-selling author of sizzling historical romance and erotic romance. While not reading, writing or researching for her latest book, she chases after her three children. In her spare time (if there is such a thing...) she likes daydreaming, wine-tasting, traveling, hiking, staring at the stars, watching movies, shopping and visiting with family and friends. She lives atop a small mountain, and enjoys cold winter nights when she can curl up in front of a roaring fire with her own knight in shining armor. Visit Eliza at www.elizaknight.com or her historical blog History Undressed: www.historyundressed.com

Made in the USA
Lexington, KY
18 October 2013